Escaping Lust
Sexy
Stories
Collection

VOLUME 4

10 EROTIC SHORT STORIES

HELANA PARKINS

Publisher's Note: This is a work of fiction. Names,
characters, places, and incidents are a product of
the author's imagination. Locales and public
names are sometimes used for atmospheric
purposes. Any resemblance to actual people, living
or dead, or to businesses, companies, events,
institutions, or locales is completely coincidental.

Escaping Lust/ Helana Parkins. -- 1st ed.
Xplicit Press, an imprint of TLM Media LLC

ISBN-13: 978-1-62327-532-7
ISBN-10: 1-62327-532-6
eISBN: 978-1-62327-585-3

Printed in the United States of America

CONTENTS

1 THE DANCER

Kelly's Secret

Daniel had been nervous all night. Since his divorce, he hadn't dated anyone else. Two years. Two years of abstinence. Tonight it felt it had been like forever. He had to change something about this. Now. But, how? Prostitute? No way; he was desperate, but not that desperate. Call a colleague and invite her for dinner? Hmmm, he couldn't think of one he found attractive. He decided to go to a night club, have some drinks, let the girls turn him on and then decide what to do about his problem.

The club didn't seem very tempting from the outside. It was a small, dark building with pink neon letters advertising "Hot

Girls, Cold Beer." He would have never set foot in this club had it not been for his friend Jamie. He had told him once about this nightclub, and had praised it.

"Man, if you want to see some real hot chicks, go to this place!" he'd said, shaking his hand as if he had burnt it.

So, there he was, in a nightclub by himself. He could feel the bass of the music in his stomach. In every corner were small stages where girls presented themselves to the men, dancing seductively in the shortest dresses he had ever seen. Some didn't even wear any, only their lingerie kept them from being completely nude.

He had to admit his friend was right. The females were extraordinarily attractive. Especially this one girl over there, in white.

Wait a second; he wiped his eyes in disbelief.

Was this really true? Or were his senses playing a joke on him? He was sure he had just recognized a hot dancer who was sensually writhing around the pole a few feet across from him. It couldn't be Kelly. Kelly – of all people! He closed his eyes to sort his thoughts.

Kelly was his student. He liked her, mostly because she was easy to handle. She was quiet and mousy, never caused any trouble. Unlike other students who showed up late for class, didn't show up at all, or never did their assignments. And usually, those students would fail every exam but, not Kelly. She exceeded most of her fellow students, regarding her grades anyway.

Her appearance, though, was closer to old-fashioned and plain. For class she wore knee-length, straight skirts that were olive green, beige or brown. This would be accompanied by a gray, blue, yellow, or black cardigan – all buttons fastened to the last one –, flat, dark brown shoes and glasses that framed her big hazel eyes and made them look even bigger.

He opened his eyes again. There, across the room, was an insanely attractive young woman crouching in front of the pole with her legs embracing the shiny metal. No way could this be Kelly.

He took a closer look at the dancer's face and added glasses in his imagination, subtracting the makeup.

Yes, it was definitely Kelly.

Stunned, he went over to the seats and mingled with the other men voraciously staring at her, following their lead.

She was gorgeous. Her long, seductive legs were adorned with white thigh-high boots that were laced on the sides. Despite the extreme height of their heels, Kelly moved her beautiful body gracefully, which was barely covered with a short, white net dress. Underneath she only wore a tiny G-string, her well-shaped breasts bare, for everyone to see.

Kelly knew how to tease the guys. Her hips continuously pushed lustfully toward the pole, to the rhythm of the suggestive music played throughout the club, her face implying high sexual excitement.

Daniel felt his throat get dry, and swallowing became increasingly difficult. He still couldn't comprehend that his plain Jane student was dancing here – for him, turning him on. Of course she didn't know that he was a spectator, but somehow it was still like she was doing all these unambiguous movements for him and for him alone.

She now turned around and presented her profile. Her upper body slowly bent forward, her legs and her butt pressing slightly against the pole. She placed her hands on her breasts as if to cover them, but this was impossible for her since they were much bigger than her hands, so she started caressing them.

Daniel didn't notice his mouth was half open. He only realized it when his throat was so dry he couldn't swallow at all. Additionally, his pants were tightening.

Embarrassed for getting so hot in public, he checked out the other men around him. Most of them had leaned back in their seats, lost in Kelly's sexy performance. No one paid attention to him. He sighed in relief and got up, ashamed that he had let himself go like this.

That night, Daniel tossed and turned but couldn't find any sleep. The girl he saw at the club would just not leave his mind.

She is my student, he tried to reason with himself. It's Kelly, for Heaven's sake!

But somehow those words completely failed their purpose. They just made him hotter.

He pictured Kelly in her everyday outfit, sitting in his class, listening to him, her legs crossed. What did she wear under her skirts? A G-string like the one she had worn tonight? And stockings? Thigh-highs? A garter belt maybe? And did she wear a bra at all?

He remembered the time he had asked her to come to the blackboard. He wanted to show the other students that at least one of them had done their homework. It was about a month ago. Was she already working at the club at that time? He remembered the blouse she wore that day and all of a sudden it occurred to him that there were no signs of a bra at all. He recalled the blouses of the other girls, but he could definitely tell they were wearing one, since he could make out the fastener and the straps. But, with Kelly... He called back the memory. It was clear and obvious – she did not wear any.

So maybe, he concluded, she also wears those tiny G-strings.

He imagined her in class, without her clothes, just with this little piece of lingerie he was so fond of.

In his pajamas he suddenly felt constricted. Quickly he pulled them off without removing his blanket. Yes, that felt much better.

In his mind, Kelly bent over, supporting her arms on a table in front of her and spreading her legs. Daniel's hand lay around his erection. He sighed softly. Kelly now climbed on the table. She sat there, on all fours, looking at him wantonly. His hand began to slowly move up and down. Now kneeling, she leaned back, pushing her breasts against each other. One of her hands slid into her G-string. Kelly caressed herself gently. Daniel's hand tightened around his cock.

She moaned and bent over again, so she would be on all fours like before. "Come here," she sighed in ecstasy, offering him her behind. Daniel started stroking himself faster. "Why don't come over here and put your hard cock in me?"

Kelly's middle finger penetrated into her. His hand went up and down again. "Oh yes, please," she sighed as her finger moved in and out of her. Daniel felt himself losing control, moaning in pleasure.

"Oh Daniel," she almost yelled. "Make me come!" "Oh yes!" With a loud groan, Daniel came, spilling himself into his hand.

And again, just like before in the club, he was embarrassed at himself when he realized the situation. He had just gotten himself off to one of his students. With a spinning head he got up and went into the bathroom to take a cold shower.

During the entire class, he had a hard time staying cool. Now that he knew her secret, she was desirable to him. No, not desirable – she was all he wanted. Sitting over there, innocently, wearing a blue cardigan, brown skirt and her glasses. Her hair was tamed by a simple rubber band and Daniel couldn't help picturing her loosening her long, shiny hair and unbuttoning her cardigan, getting ready for work.

Work, he repeated to himself, smiling. Was it really work for her or did she enjoy it?

Kelly looked up from her notepad and right in his direction. Daniel flushed. He had been staring at her for at several minutes; no wonder she wanted to know what that was about.

He quickly turned away and continued teaching, unable to get his mind off her.

Later that night, he went to the club again to see her. But to his disappointment, she was not there. Instead he returned home, sank into his sofa and half-heartedly turned on the TV. While some talk show host was babbling, Daniel's thoughts went back to Kelly. This time he pictured her in this awesome white net dress and boots. Were they latex? Possibly, since they were so shiny and tight. Oh, the way she had moved her hips! As if the cool, metallic pole offered her sexual gratification. Quick, intense pushes.

Daniel unwittingly unzipped his pants and let them slide down to his ankles, along with his boxers. He briefly looked at his hardness and wished Kelly would do the same with him as she did with the pole. He wanted her to slowly sit down on his lap, letting his member carefully glide into her. Oh, how warm and tight she was!

His hand started stroking his hard erection. Up and down it moved, just like Kelly would do, riding him, doing it harder and faster every second. He could almost feel it going in and out of her. She would touch her incredible breasts, the same way she had done on stage, but this time she would do it only for him, and this time her tongue would caress them, too.

His fist pounded up and down in a frenzy, his pelvis supporting every movement.

"Next time I see you," he yelled, "I will tear off your clothes and fuck you."

Gasping and moaning, he came all over his hand.

Daniel had asked Kelly stay longer after class. This was the third time in two weeks. Since she was a great student who never made any trouble, he had to use all of his imagination to come up with a good and believable explanation for keeping her. This time he told her he had seen her cheat on a test. Of course it was not true, but it was the only way he could be alone with her. So far he hadn't tried anything. It just felt good to punish her a little. After all it was her fault he had to fool with himself every night. Last night it was even two times! That deserved punishment.

"I really didn't cheat," she protested.

"Stop it!" Daniel was surprised by how

harsh he was with her. "You know what you did. Don't play innocent!"

"But really, Mr. Smith! I promise, I didn't..."

Her sweet voice, her big eyes and all those images in his head were just too much for him. He stepped up to Kelly and made her get up.

"I've seen you, you know," he whispered. "At work." He waited a moment for her reaction, which consisted of a questioning look.

"You are an incredibly good dancer," he hinted.

Now she understood. Her eyes widened and her cheeks turned deep red.

Daniel leaned forward so he could whisper in her ear. "I won't tell anybody... if I can fuck you."

He let it sink in with her for a while before he continued.

"I want it here. Now. Rough and intense."

She didn't say anything. Instead she started unbuttoning her cardigan.

Daniel smiled in excitement. At last he would get the girl.

So she doesn't wear anything under her clothes, he noted, as she stood in front of him, her skirt and cardigan on the floor.

"Bend over," he ordered in a military tone.

She obeyed, putting her hands on the

table for support.

Daniel hurried to get his pants off. He couldn't wait any longer, he was already so hard. There she was, the girl he had fantasized about, right in front of him, willing to please. He stepped behind her and grasping her hips, thrust himself into her. She gave a sigh and opened her legs a little more.

"You will pay for making me so horny."

Breathing heavily and loudly, he went in and out of her. Daniel was not the least bit careful, he just wanted relief, and he would only attain it through fucking her as hard as he could.

Kelly lifted her leg and put her knee on the table. This way Daniel could go deeper into her. "Oh yes," he groaned in approval.

His right hand pulled her hip toward him, while his left hand began to spank her.

"This is for making me hard at the club." He thrust into her as he slapped her ass.

Kelly started to moan, too.

"Oh," Daniel growled, pleasantly surprised. "You like this, do you?"

He spanked her again. Another sigh.

"I like it, too," he grunted, spanking her several times. A red print of his hand appeared on her butt.

She extended it towards him even more.

Daniel pushed harder into her, his hand

sliding between her legs. With every thrust she rubbed her clit against his hand. Her breathing quickened and he could tell she was going to come.

"Don't you dare scream," he hissed.

Frantic with pleasure, she just begged, "Faster, please, faster."

He slammed into her violently.

"You'd better hurry up," he moaned, "I'm going to come all inside you real soon." No sooner had he said this than he felt her ecstatic convulsions pulsating around his member.

"Such a good girl," he gasped, emptying himself inside of her with an explosion.

He had never felt better when he put on his pants again and adjusted his shirt. Nevertheless, he didn't really know what to say to Kelly. Thank you? I hope you enjoyed it as much as I did? It all seemed unfitting.

Fortunately, Kelly spoke up. "I actually liked it," she commented like she was talking about a movie or a meal. "This was the best sex I've had in a while."

Daniel was dumbfounded. How much sex did she have per week, per month, per year?

She smiled. "So, will you keep my secret now?"

He thought for a moment. If he agreed, then it was over. No more Kelly. He couldn't let that happen.

"Well," he began and looked straight into her eyes. "I will. If you pay me a visit now and then."

Kelly had to laugh. "I could think of worse conditions for a contract. So, let's say you keep your mouth shut and you can bang me as often as you want."

Daniel returned her laugh and unbuckled his belt again. "Why don't we start now then? I've got a lot of catching up to do."

Kelly got on her knees, smiling. "Whatever you wish, Professor Smith."

2 ONE FIRST FOR THE LAST TIME

Jack hung his jacket on the coat rack and examined his office spiritlessly. He had the biggest office the company had to offer, and he had worked for years to get here. To him, it seemed like an eternity. All his life had flashed by and he hadn't even noticed. But now that his fortieth birthday had passed, he was questioning his decision to completely focus on his job and neglect every other aspect of his existence. To be honest, he not only questioned it but regretted it.

What had he missed? More than a decade of football games, movies, theater plays, concerts. He even failed to show up at his daughter's ballet performances, as well as his son's tennis matches. Ballet and tennis. He shook his head. His wife and he knew that Josh would have rather played baseball but they thought, as the son of the manager of Whiteman & Forms, he should do something more sophisticated. Was Josh happy with this decision? Jack couldn't tell. But how could he? He was at the office from 8 AM to 8 PM, so he didn't see much of his family. Let alone of Barbara.

They had been married for 20 years now. What a milestone! But that was all there was to say about him and Barbara. She was more interested in her book club than in him. The book club! Jack hated it with a passion. All her snobbish friends would come over for tea and they would talk about the latest schmaltzy book they had read. It was always the same. Man and woman meet. They fall in love. Something happens to prevent them from being together. They both suffer. Then, a happy turn of events and in the end all is well and they have sex.

Barbara had once made him read one of those novels. The detailed sex scenes had made him hot and he reached over to the other side of the bed where Barbara was lying. He started kissing her but she just pushed him away, saying she didn't want to be intimate at the moment.

Now, this statement made him laugh bitterly as he remembered it. This "moment" had lasted three years now.

Jack was simply frustrated. Was he still a man? An attractive man? He knew in his twenties he could have gotten any woman he wanted. And he did. Until he met Barbara. She was the love of his life, and he loved her still. But the sex... She wasn't interested anymore. He, on the other hand, needed it. He needed it badly.

A friend of his told him one night at a bar, during their "guy's night," about a website that brokered affairs. It was for people who were married or in a relationship but missed the fun in it. That night Jack had rejected this idea vigorously. But this morning it had popped back into his mind and he couldn't stop thinking about it. With the intention to just look around and feed his curiosity, he sank into his office chair and typed in the web address.

What a disappointment! He raised his hands in resignation. It wasn't possible to surf the website unless you were a member and logged in.

Well, I could, he pondered. Should I?

His hands hovered over the keyboard. He wouldn't have to reveal his real name, he reasoned with himself. He could use a nickname like... like...

He had never been very creative. The more he thought about a possible name, the more he wished he had some of Barbara's creativity.

Barbara! His hands jerked back.

I can't do this!

But his mind would not be still.

All I want is just a look, nothing more. There's nothing wrong with that, is there?

"No," he replied to himself loudly and smiled confidently.

But what name? Snoopy, like his favorite cartoon dog? No, already taken. He is a Beagle, so "Beagle." This, too, was taken.

Okay, what about MrBeagles?

Jack typed it and this time was successful.

Over the next hour Jack browsed the catalogue of potential sex partners. One profile in particular caught his attention. It was the profile of a 25-year-old, she called herself CuteBunny, and man, he had to admit that she definitely was cute. And extremely hot.

The picture she had posted showed a slim girl with long, fiery red hair. Definitely dyed, a glaring color like that couldn't possibly be natural. In the picture she wore a black top that looked like a corsage; it pushed her breasts up, pressing half of them out of the top. The rest of her was only covered by an extraordinarily short skirt.

Jack got lost in this image. He imagined touching this young woman, holding her in his arms, loving her over and over again until they both were completely exhausted.

Why don't you message her? A voice popped up in his head.

He wiped it away. Just looking, that was all he wanted to do.

But, he started debating again, but if I write her and she's interested, maybe we can exchange some hot mails. That's allowed for a married man, isn't it?

He was still thinking this thought as he composed a message to her and hit the send button.

Excitedly smiling, he leaned back in his chair. All he could do now was wait.

But no! She already had written back!

With a shaky hand he opened the mail.

"I'm glad you like my photo! But what about yours? I would like to see who I'm talking to."

She wanted a picture? Hastily, Jack looked through his folders for a decent one.

Yes, this was a pretty good one; it showed him in a dress shirt, confidently smiling. Quickly he attached it to his next message to CuteBunny and mailed it.

He didn't have to wait long for her response.

"Wow," she wrote. "You're exactly my type! Are you married?"

Jack told her everything about his marriage, about his kids, his job and his need. According to her messages, she was in a similar situation, only that she was a housewife and her husband neglected her because of his job. She seemed very frustrated, almost as frustrated as him.

"I dream of a man who knows what he wants from me," she let him know. "I want this man to seduce me and do me all night long."

Jack's heart started beating faster in excitement as he read these lines. "Well, baby, let me be this man. I'm in so much need one night wouldn't be enough."

"Why don't you come over?" she suggested. "I'm alone, and I want it so much right now. Can you help me?"

Jack's thoughts all whirled around. He couldn't believe this girl wanted him. Well, he wanted her, too. But he couldn't leave work. That would be too suspicious. He told her that.

"Too bad," was her reply. "I guess I'll have to help myself."

Whoa, what? Jack's eyes got big as her words sank in.

"What are you going to do?" he inquired, hoping his assumption was right.

"There is this toy I have," she explained, making his mind come up with the hottest images of her playing with it. He could feel the effect of those pictures in his pants. "I'm holding it in my left hand. It's big and hard. After I send this message to you, I'm going to put it in me."

Jack sat there, staring at the screen. Was she really playing with herself now? Right this moment? He needed to know. The tightness of his pants needed to know.

"Is it in you? How does it feel?"

"Yes, it's in me. I'm moving it in and out of me, slowly, like you would move in and out of me. How I wish you were here."

Jack was so aroused that he had to do something. He unzipped his pants to let his hand slide in. His erection was huge.

"I want to be in the place of your toy. If you only knew how hard I am right now."

"I wish you were in its place," CuteBunny told him. "It's going in me rough and fast. It feels so good."

Reading these lines, Jack automatically began to stroke his hardness. Oh yes, it felt so good. But it would definitely feel better if he were in her mouth and could watch her sliding that toy into herself at the same time. He told her.

"I would blow you so intensely," she promised. "Oh, just the thought of it drives me crazy. I'm doing myself so hard. I really need it, MrBeagles."

Good God, his voice cried out in his head, his hand moving furiously inside his pants. He barely managed to type with his free hand.

"Believe me, I desperately want to fuck you. You've made me so horny I'm about to come in my pants."

And this wasn't understated. With some energetic movements of his hand he exploded. White liquid ran over his hands and wet his pants.

They had been chatting for weeks. Finally, Jack felt balanced again. There was a girl who was crazy about him, and this made him excited. He couldn't recall the last time he felt this way. Now it was time to meet in person.

Barbara didn't suspect anything when he left early this morning. She probably thought he was going to work. They hadn't talked in two days. He couldn't tell why. Maybe they just had nothing to say to each other. Jack turned into a side road. There it was! Just like she had described it. Right in front of him was a small motel.

He stopped in the empty parking lot and got out of the car. Yes, it was empty, except for one other car. Was it hers? His heart started to race. Was she already waiting for him? What would he do if they saw each other? Was he supposed to take her right away? And, most importantly, would he be able to cheat on his wife? Up until now it was just playing but if he went ahead and did what he promised CuteBunny, his conscience would not be clean anymore.

Well, it isn't anyway, he calmed himself down. What I have told this girl isn't innocent at all.

He grinned, lost in thoughts. No, it wasn't innocent. He had told her in detail how he would do her, how long he would do her and how often. He had shared his most intimate moments with her, namely when he got himself off. But she had done the same thing. With her toy...

"Mmmh," he murmured quietly at this thought. What was he waiting for?

At the check-in desk he picked up the key to the room. The second one, he was told, had already been picked up by a red-haired lady. Jack's knees felt like jelly. Slowly he walked toward the door with the number 24. His hand trembled as he turned the knob. Immediately, his eye caught the bed that was straight across from the door. On it, CuteBunny was waiting for him, wearing a see-through baby doll.

"Hello MrBeagles," she breathed. "Why don't you join me?"

He felt something rise in his pants. Obediently, he walked over to the bed and sat down.

"My name is actually..."

She gently placed her finger on his lips.

"Don't tell me," she whispered as she began to kiss his neck. "To me you will always be MrBeagles." He closed his eyes since she climbed on his lap, kissing his chin tenderly.

"You know, you're making MrBeagles lose his mind."

"Good," she responded, before he grabbed her and kissed her lips passionately.

His hand slid under the baby doll to grasp her butt.

"Oh, I can feel something," she teased, letting her fingers glide between his legs.

"Yeah," he gasped. "You always make it hard."

She smiled sweetly as she started to move her hips rhythmically on his lap. "I hope so." Her hands kneaded her big breasts through the black fabric.

Jack was out of his mind. "You don't know what you're doing." His pelvis automatically pushed against her, adjusting to her rhythm. Her response was a sassy smile, followed by a deep kiss while she was still teasing him with the movement of her hips. Jack let one of his hands slip from her butt further down. He could feel she was already very aroused. Softly he began to rub her.

She moaned and moved faster. "I want to have you in me," she demanded.

His index finger gently penetrated into her. "Like this?" he grinned.

He got his answer by her moving up and down on his finger.

"Oh, you do like this," he mumbled, enjoying it himself.

"Yes," she groaned. "Don't stop!" Her nails dug deep in his shoulder, increasing the speed of her rhythm even more. Jack literally lent her a hand by giving her more fingers. Fascinated, he watched her as her ecstasy was growing.

"Oh God!" she exclaimed and froze in her movements. Every inch of her body was shaking. Jack wouldn't let her rest, and he wanted his share. He laid her on the bed and turned her around, so that she was lying on her stomach. Frantically he got rid of his pants.

"Show me your butt," he ordered throaty.

She presented it to him by getting on her knees while keeping her chest on the bed.

He harshly grabbed her hips, thrusting his member into her with a loud sigh.

"Oh please, fuck me hard," she moaned.

"You bet," Jack hissed.

He pushed so roughly into her that it only took a few minutes until she climaxed again. He could feel her coming, her tightening around him.

It made it hard for him to last much longer. With an intense groan he burst within her. It took several convulsions until he was absolutely empty.

Exhausted, he fell onto the pillows.

"What's wrong, MrBeagles?" CuteBunny wanted to know, cuddling up to him. "Already worn out? I could do with some more of your incredible best friend." Her hand stroked his cock.

"Give me a short break, honey." He smiled satisfactorily. "We have all day and almost all night."

He put his arm around her. Barbara wouldn't care if he came home a little later, since it wasn't that unusual for him. Somehow he was surprised by how easy it actually was to cheat on her. He didn't feel any remorse, just the opposite.

But that would probably change as soon as he returned home. And this he would do. Return. Return to his life as a manager; as the husband of a woman who didn't see him as a man anymore; as the father of two kids his wife had raised to become two little snobs; as a man who met his buddies every Thursday night at the bar for a couple of drinks. He would return, and so would she, keeping the memory of these few hours of absolute sexual fulfillment in the back chamber of their minds. Knowing they got to live their fantasies for one day. Knowing it wouldn't survive the next morning. For fantasies are nothing but desires that, once met, can't be special every day, except for this one day – where the first time becomes the last time.

3 HER FAVORITE CLASS

Sadie quietly unpacked her bag, piling the books neatly with the notepad. The last item to be placed on top of this pile was a small, colorful pencil case. She opened it and fished a purple pen out to keep her hand busy. Before she had entered the classroom, she had gone to the bathroom, which she actually hated because of all the dirt and filth. But today was different. Today she needed to check her make up and her hair, her appearance in general, before going to class. Today was Tuesday. It was the day of her English class with Mr. James Rayne. Her favorite class. Her favorite professor.

She had to smile. "Professor" - that sounded so old! Mr. Rayne wasn't old at all. In fact, he was about her age, around 25, maybe a few years older. And he was so hot! All the girls in this class adored him, not to mention his other classes. The seminar she was attending was packed with young female students, trying to get Mr. Rayne's attention. And she knew from friends that his afternoon classes and the classes on Thursday were crowded with admirers as well. And they were all so pretty! Sadie was aware that he had the agony of choice and she felt she could not keep up with their beauty. But, she knew she was clever – so she'd have to resort to some tricks if she wanted to have him.

And she did want him! The first time she saw him it felt like lightning had just struck her. He looked exactly like the man she had always dreamed of. It was as if her imaginary lover had come to life and now stood before her. She loved blue eyes, and his eyes were the purest, piercing blue eyes she had ever seen. No girl could resist his look. Including her. And this was her biggest problem. She had too much competition.

She looked up from the pen she was toying with and examined the classroom carefully. By now it had become crowded with dolled up girls, prancing across the room, presenting their short skirts, and even shorter tops. Automatically she lowered her eyes to look at her outfit. A shirt and jeans. Okay, the jeans were pretty tight, showing off her curves, as well as the shirt, but this did not even meet half of the points the other girls met on an attraction scale.

Maybe she could put on some more lip gloss? No, too late, he just entered the room. She could feel his presence, even if she didn't raise her head. Her heart started to beat faster.

"Good morning," he greeted his students merrily, dropping some books on his desk.

Her heart raced. Still, she kept her head low.

"First, the attendance list." She heard a muffled sound and knew he had sat down on the table with the list in his hand, as he always did.

"Nancy," he read the first name.

"Yes," she breathed back.

Nancy, she thought angrily. You won't get him, so stop trying to hit on him so bluntly! It's embarrassing!

She hated Nancy with all her heart. She didn't know her very well, but the fact that she was beautiful and sexy was reason enough to loathe her. She was every man's ideal – tall, slim, long blonde hair, and dressed like a Barbie doll. She actually resembled Barbie, a little. And her all too obvious Barbie doll advances, her almost moaned "Yes" made Sadie's blood boil in jealousy.

"Sadie?"

In her silent rage she had almost failed to hear her own name.

"Yes."

Her cheeks blushed as she noticed that her "Yes" wasn't any better than Nancy's. Both girls exchanged a hateful look which Mr. Rayne didn't seem to notice.

Of course he didn't see it, Sadie sadly noted to herself. He won't waste time looking at me.

She spent the following 87 minutes wallowing in her depressing thoughts but at the end of class she suddenly gained new hope, making her heart jump.

"For those of you who need some extra hours studying for the exam, I'm offering a study group every Wednesday night at 8 PM."

A study group! Perfect! She could see him off campus! But wait, she tempered her enthusiasm. Where is the study group taking place? She almost panicked when she realized she had to ask him about this. But why was she so afraid? Didn't she want his attention? So, the first step to get it would be to step up and talk to him.

She took a deep breath and slowly walked towards his desk, focusing on every single step. The sound of her heels echoed through the room that was now almost empty, except for the obligatory girls that were fanatically pursuing their goal – namely to have Mr. Rayne for themselves.

My shoes are too loud, Sadie quietly thought to herself, as she noticed the attention she drew because of them.

Her professor and the girls gathered around him, including Nancy, were looking at her. His eyes seemed rather surprised but friendly, while her fellow students all gave her a disapproving look.

"Hey Sadie," he addressed her kindly. "How can I help you?"

She was trembling and trying not to show it, especially not in her voice. As firmly as she could, she replied. "Where does the study group take place?"

"Oh." His eyes widened. "You? You want to participate?"

"Um..." She felt her cheeks turn deep red. "Well... I thought..."

Maybe he could sense her insecurity, since he smiled encouragingly. "I didn't mean you couldn't come. I'm just surprised because you are such a good student."

"Thank you," she whispered. Her head hung low, her eyes staring at the ground. "But I need some help."

"Well, it will be at my place. Here's the address." He scribbled something on a small piece of paper and handed it to her.

"See you tomorrow then." He gave her a sweet smile, making her blush even more.

Sadie wasn't able to return the smile; she just turned around and left.

She had spent hours in front of the mirror, changing several times until she decided on her favorite pair of black jeans and a pretty, light blue shirt that emphasized her feminine body. Her dark hair fell loose over her shoulders, supporting her girlish look.

Sadie knew Nancy would show up too, and she would most certainly be dressed in one of her Barbie dresses. Sadie was sure she was just no match for Nancy; if he would ever choose one of his students, Mr. Rayne would choose Nancy. But she at least wanted to try to make him see her, the small, quiet, plain Jane.

"What are the odds?" she asked her reflection in the mirror as if she really expected an answer. With a sigh of frustration she grabbed her lip gloss and applied it to her lips, making them shimmer lightly.

When she arrived at Mr. Rayne's place, she was embarrassed to learn she was the last one. Everyone had been waiting for her in the living room.

Apologizing, she squeezed herself on the couch between Nora and Gina, two girls she liked. Nonetheless, even they were rivals.

Sadie couldn't tell what happened during the next hour. She was too preoccupied with the thought that she was in his house, that he was sitting only a few feet away. He was so close she could have touched him if she had wanted to. Well, she indeed had wanted to, but in front of everyone else? And anyway, she wasn't the type of girl who would do something so bold.

She only woke up from her daydreams when everyone else around her was getting up and leaving. One after the other, the girls filed past him, stopping briefly to give him their hands, to flirt.

Sadie watched them, disappointed that it was already over.

"And you?" He smiled, causing Sadie's heart to stop for a second. "Still need help?"

She wasn't sure if he was serious or just joking but this could be her chance! She would just have to make up a problem related to class and she might be able to be around him longer!

"Well," she began, as she always did when she was insecure and not sure what to say.

Mr. Rayne's smile got bigger. "Yes?" He

waited for an answer.

"The problem is..." She lost herself in his stunningly blue eyes.

"Okay?" He seemed to be amused by her shyness and her inability to come up with a topic she didn't understand and sat down next to her, curiously awaiting her next words.

He was so close now! Sadie could smell his aftershave, a very masculine scent. His eyes didn't let go of her; instead, they were wandering across her face, stopping shortly at her mouth, just to move upwards to her eyes again. She held his gaze, feeling her blood pumping through her vessels with more and more pressure. She bet her cheeks, or actually her entire face, was visibly flooded with blood now. Breathing got harder too; her chest moved up and down in short intervals.

Mr. Rayne's smile froze.

Oh no! Sadie's alarm bells went off. Does he know? Have I just given myself away?

She tried to read the answer in his expression. But he just stared into her eyes.

How could she get out of this situation? Get up and leave?

No, she wouldn't do that. It would make things worse. Next week in class she would feel so ashamed.

Okay, how about finally coming up with

a question?

She tried as hard as she could but his gaze prevented her from having even one clear thought.

Her body longed to be in his arms, to feel his kisses, to feel his hands all over her. And he was just right beside her, his arms in reach, she would just have to cozy up a bit and she could feel his body against hers.

"So?" He pulled her back into real life. His voice sounded rough, not as friendly as it was before.

Maybe leaving is the best option after all. With these thoughts she got up, intending to politely say goodbye and go home. But he held her wrist and pulled her back to the couch.

Surprised and a little scared, she listened to his words.

"Don't bother. I think I know what's wrong. Just tell me..." He paused for a few seconds before he continued in a low voice. "Is it true?"

"I-is what true?" she stuttered, her heart racing so fast she thought it would explode any moment.

"Is it true..." He stopped to place his index finger under her chin to lift it up. His face was so close to hers now that she could feel his breath on her skin.

Sadie couldn't wait until he had finished his sentence. She suddenly lost her shyness, she lost all her doubts and fears. She just knew she wanted him. Now. She would deal with the consequences later.

Closing her eyes, she leaned forward and let her lips touch his.

She expected he would push her away, telling her that she was his student and that he had to be professional. But it didn't happen. Just the opposite. He kissed her back, wrapping his arms tightly around her.

Sadie was in seventh heaven. The man she had desired for months was holding her in his arms, kissing her passionately.

She pressed her body against his, making him sigh quietly. "What are you doing, Sadie?" he whispered, enjoying her touch.

She kissed his neck before she breathed the answer into his ear. "I want you."

His response was clear. He pulled her onto his lap, his tongue heatedly seeking hers.

Sadie could feel he was aroused. She wished she could make the fabric between her and him disappear, and inevitably began to press herself against his hard erection. Her yearning movements made him moan in pleasure, his hand slipping under her shirt, feeling her breasts. His other hand slid across her back, down to her ass, increasing the pressure she applied on his lap, making her move faster.

Sadie put her head back and gave a deep sigh. His hands made her so hot and the emotions she had kept to herself for so long overwhelmed her in one big wave, she forgot about any inhibitions.

"I want this..." Her hand fell into his lap, embracing his member through his pants. "...to be in me."

Motionless he stared at her for a moment.

"Put it in me," she begged, her hand slowly moving in his lap. "Please."

With one energetic move of his hand he ripped the fine fabric that once was Sadie's shirt off her body. Her bra was next.

"Do you know I've had dreams about this?" he asked breathlessly as Sadie was sitting on his lap, topless.

"About what?" she asked.

"About me, doing you just like this."

"Me?" Sadie couldn't believe what she just heard.

"Yes, you. Your body has given me wet dreams since the first class we had together." His hungry eyes examined her breasts in detail. "Let's make it a reality."

Sadie was so taken by surprise that she didn't notice much of his getting rid of her pants. She was only fully aware again of what was happening when he laid on top of her. They were both on the floor; she didn't know how they got there, she just knew she didn't want to wait any longer.

"Fuck me," she pleaded almost inaudibly.

"Oh girl, you bet," he responded with heavy breathing, unzipping his pants. "This is for all the countless times you made me hard during class."

She could feel his erection hard against her, without fabric between them. She lifted her hips to make it easier for him, and carefully he slid into her.

"Oh God," she exclaimed when he was as deep in her as it was possible.

Slowly he began to move inside her, making her gasp.

"Fuck me harder," she begged, gliding her hands across his back.

He pushed faster in and out of her, while she put her legs around him, allowing him to penetrate even deeper.

Sadie could feel him get even harder.

"I'm about to come," he groaned in pleasure. "I'm about to..." She felt hot liquid being pushed deep into her, as her professor was pressing himself against her, moaning and breathing heavily.

This turned her on so much that her hand almost automatically moved between her legs where it began to stimulate her.

Fascinated, but still recovering from his orgasm, he watched her facial expression.

Sadie got more and more excited, sighing and whispering his name. After a while she could feel him get hard inside her again.

"Oh please," she begged, "make me come!"

His response was several hard and rough pushes.

She could feel her climax coming, like a huge wave getting closer each time he thrust it into her.

"Oh... Oh James... Oh God James!"

The wave rolled through her entire body, making her tremble in ecstasy, her fingernails scratching his back and neck. At that moment he, too, did came again.

Sadie hadn't heard from her professor since they had shared that hot evening together. And she did not want to chase after a man, so she had just waited. What was wrong? Did he not want her anymore? Well, she would find out in a few minutes.

Lost in thought, she was chewing on her pen when Mr. Rayne entered the classroom. Her heart stood still. Would he give her a sign? A look, a wink, a smile, anything?

She waited for this to happen the whole session. Nothing. She was convinced that he had just used her when he suddenly addressed her and told her to come to his office this afternoon.

She was there on time, excited and nervous.

"Hey," he smiled as he saw her standing in the door. "Come on in!"

No sooner had she closed the door behind herself than she found herself in his arms.

"I missed you," he chided gently.

Confused, Sadie attempted to ask why she hadn't heard from him, but he covered her mouth with his lips, kissing her deeply.

Her knees got weak, she had to hold on to him and wrapped her arms around his neck.

"I don't know how you do this but whenever I see you, or even think of you, I get so hot." He led her hand between his legs so she could feel his hardness.

Sadie felt hot too. He had such huge power over her and she just wanted to please him, to make him moan again, to make him tell her hot things again.

She removed his belt and unfastened his pants so they – together with his underwear – slid down.

"Sit down," she murmured and showed him by slightly lifting her skirt that she wasn't wearing anything underneath.

He did as he was told and watched her

while she slowly sat down on his hard member. He sighed loudly and began to guide the movement of her hips with his hands.

She was so turned on by this situation – sitting on her professor's lap in his office, feeling him so hard and deep in her – that it didn't take long until she came. He apparently felt the same, since his orgasm was almost simultaneous.

"Will you come to my office again tomorrow morning?" he asked while they both were rearranging their clothes.

"Of course," Sadie promised. "I can't wait."

4 WILL YOU BE MY HOSTAGE?

"Sit down and keep your mouth shut," Charlie ordered harshly, pointing at a corner of the shabby apartment they had just entered.

Katherine didn't move, so he pushed her toward the corner, making her fall. Her hands were still tied behind her back, making movement difficult but she eventually managed to sit up and rest her head and shoulders against the wall.

"You stay there, you understand?" Charlie hissed. He waited for her to nod before turning around and joining his accomplice, who was sitting on a couch and looking at the contents of a duffel bag.

"How much did we get?" Charlie asked impatiently.

Red looked at him and grinned.

"Enough."

Both men laughed, shaking off the tension and nervousness of the past few hours. Earlier that day they had finally gone through with their plan to rob a bank. Everything was so thoroughly planned out that they had not expected anything to go wrong. But it did. One of the tellers must have pushed an emergency button which neither Red nor Charlie had noticed. The police arrived much too soon so they were compelled to leave half of the money behind, but they still had managed to get out with a hostage.

The hostage happened to be twenty-seven year old bank teller Katherine, who'd had the bad luck to kneel, trembling with fear, right next to Charlie. He didn't think about it, he just grabbed her by her arm and used her as a shield in case the police decided to shoot them. But no shot was fired. As soon as the policemen saw the woman, they lowered their guns, and Red, Charlie and Katherine were able to leave the crime scene unharmed in her car.

She tried to sit still, although the rope around her wrists cut into her skin and left her in pain. She watched the two men sitting on the couch; they were busy counting the stacks of cash they had made away with.

One of them was tall, with short black hair; he seemed to be pretty strong. Although he wore a blue long sleeve shirt, she could make out the well-defined muscles of his arms and stomach. He was the guy who had taken her hostage. Without warning he had pulled her up from the floor, his grip tight around her arm. She was scared to death as he jabbed the gun into her back, pushing her forward. Fear had numbed all her senses; she just put one foot in front of the other and moved toward the car.

She couldn't tell how long the drive had been, but to her it seemed like an eternity. When they finally stopped, the guy with black hair, Charlie, had dragged her out of the vehicle and into a run-down building which looked more like a flophouse than anything else. Charlie had pushed her inside a door.

"Please, don't hurt me," she begged, terrified.

"Sit down and keep your mouth shut," were the harsh words that served as a response.

Katherine had been too afraid to move, so she just kept staring at the dirty floor. The floorboards once must have been a warm brown. Some tiny spots still showed the original grain but dirt and dust must have eaten into the wood, since the planks were now mostly black. The yellowish wallpaper peeled down and hung loose on the walls.

Suddenly someone struck Katherine on her back and the next moment she was lying on the floor. She struggled to get up again; she really didn't want to touch the filthy floor with the skin of her face. It was bad enough she had to sit there.

"You stay there, you understand?" the man said, and she automatically nodded to avoid further violence.

As they walked across the room, she had some time to collect her thoughts while she watched the two men. The one called Red was a little smaller than his friend. His blonde hair was longer; it covered almost half of his ears. His muscles weren't as obvious, but nevertheless, he displayed them by wearing a tight-fitting T-Shirt.

Katherine shocked herself by thinking that they both were pretty attractive. She wondered how she was able to think of something like that in her situation. They had just taken her hostage, thrown her into a dark and filthy corner, and God knew what they would do with her later on. After all, they didn't seem like they would mind getting rid of her... for good.

At that moment, Charlie looked over to her. A shiver ran down her spine. He got up and crossed the room. She began to tremble. Was this it? Was she going to die now?

He stopped right in front of her and crouched down. "What are you looking at, huh?" His anger was audible.

Catherine could not bring herself to utter one single word, so she just stared into his bright eyes, expecting the worst.

"What are you looking at?" he yelled as his hand reached for her throat. "Stop staring at me, bitch!"

He shouted so loud, Katherine's ears hurt. His grip got tighter, making it hard for her to breathe. That's it, she thought. A tear ran down her cheek.

She just wouldn't stop staring! It was irritating. Her eyes had this sad look that really got to him. It made him feel guilty, like he was a bad man. But he wasn't bad. He had reasons for what Red and he had done, which she of course didn't know about. And a hostage! That was never part of the plan. They just wanted to get into the bank, get the money, and get out again. But now they had this girl with them. What were they supposed to do with her? Let her go? No. She would talk. Maybe not today or tomorrow, but she would eventually talk, and that made things difficult. She had to remain silent. But killing her wasn't an option either. Until they figured something out, she would have to stay with them. And go on making him feel miserable with her big sad eyes.

"Stop it!" He lost control over his voice.

In response to his own shouting, he tightened his grip around the girl's neck. He watched her eyes get even bigger in terror and her breathing get harder, her rib cage quickly moving up and down.

Charlie let go.

"What are you doing, man?" Red stepped up from behind.

"She's..." He stopped and turned around to face his buddy, still crouching. "She's irritating me."

Red sighed understandingly. "I know, man. But don't lose it, okay? We aren't killers." He eyed his friend carefully before continuing. "I'm going to go hide some of the money. You think you can handle this here by yourself?"

Charlie turned to Katherine again. She was still in shock. "Yeah, sure."

Red just nodded, took some bundles of bills and closed the door from the outside.

Charlie examined the girl carefully. She was pretty. Her long curly hair framed her cute, slightly tanned face perfectly. Freckles covered her nose and cheeks. But the latter were as pale as death. Her green eyes were watery as her full lips stuttered out a question.

"Will you kill me?" Her voice was trembling.

He had to smile. "No," he reassured her. "We aren't killers, like Red said. But you need to understand that you have to stay tied up. We can't let you run away. You might talk."

"I won't," she hastily replied.

Charlie grinned now. "Of course not." He got up. "You want something to drink?"

Katherine only nodded and his eyes went over her body before he went to fetch a glass of water. She's hot, he noted to himself. I made a good choice settling for her as a hostage. Nice to look at. With these thoughts, he handed Katherine the water.

"Oh, that's right," he said. "Forgot you can't use your hands. Well, I'll feed you then."

He lifted the glass up to her mouth and poured the water into it. But Katherine didn't drink as fast so the water ran down her chin and neck to her blouse, making it see-through. Charlie stared at it in amazement. He couldn't believe what this stain revealed. She wasn't wearing a bra. Her nipples were clearly visible through the light fabric and they were hard. I could touch them and she wouldn't be able to do anything about it.

His own thoughts surprised him, but that didn't stop his cock from getting hard.

Why did he stare at her so intensely? She followed his gaze only to see that her blouse now revealed more than it covered. She felt the blood rushing to her cheeks. How embarrassing!

She looked back at him to check his reaction. This guy was staring at her like she was his prey. Hungrily, longingly. The muscles on his arms twitched as if they were getting ready for the final attack, when his arms would close around her, pressing her against his body. She lowered her eyes so she could see his chest. Although covered, she could tell he worked out on a regular basis. Weight training, she was sure of it. Beneath the hard chest was an equally hard stomach.

She lowered her gaze further. Besides his chest and stomach, something else was hard as well. Inevitably, her lips opened a little as she felt butterflies violently fluttering around in her belly. She couldn't tell why but the man and the entire situation were starting to turn her on.

Charlie had apparently noticed that his excitement was mutual, since his face got closer to hers.

"I promise," he mumbled. "I promise I won't hurt you. Say no and I'll stop."

In response, Katherine closed her eyes and offered him her lips. She could feel his strong arms wrap around her waist, pulling her to him. In that moment the weirdest thing happened – she felt safe and secure. She was his hostage, she shouldn't feel this way, she knew this. But nonetheless, she couldn't help it.

His warm lips covered hers for a long, deep kiss. She thought she was falling. The intensity of this one kiss left her limp in his arms.

Now you can do with me whatever you desire, she thought. His kisses were filled with emotion, with such passion and yearning that Katherine, even if she wanted to, could not hold back her longing. She returned his kisses as deeply. Suddenly she felt his hand on her blouse. She moaned softly and arched her back, offering him her breasts. He responded with a sigh and began to play with her full curves. She willingly let it happen and put her head back. The sensation of every gentle touch made her breathe heavier and made her long for more. Slowly he unbuttoned her blouse, caressing the skin of her neck with his lips.

She attempted to touch him too, but was painfully stopped by the rope around her wrists. She bit her lips and groaned in pain.

"Sorry, baby," Charlie whispered breathlessly into her ear. "I can't untie you."

His warm, loving voice had a soothing effect on her, so she forgot about the hurt instantly.

"I want to feel you." Katherine was startled. Had she really said that? It must have escaped her. She tried to read the expression in Charlie's face.

He smiled teasingly. "I can arrange that."

Picking her up in his strong, muscular arms, he carried her into another room where a bed was waiting.

She was lying before him, without any irritating clothing distracting his view. Her body was gorgeous, just perfect. He wanted her so bad. And she wanted him, that's what she said a minute ago. She asked him to do her, and that's what she would get. So what was he waiting for?

Eagerly he got rid of his shirt and pants

and covered her body with his. As he thrust his erection into her, they both moaned in pleasure. He felt so good inside her and the fact that she was all tied up made it even more exciting. He moved in and out of her, breathing hard and caressing her breasts with his hands.

"Harder," she begged.

When Red returned to the apartment he heard loud moaning coming out of the bedroom. In disbelief he shook his head and went to check, mumbling, "You're not fucking our hostage, Charlie, are you?"

Charlie was.

When Red came into the room, Charlie was on top of the girl, moving up and down. Both of her legs were cocked. The sight of his friend doing the girl aroused him. As he kept watching Charlie's thrusts became faster and more forceful. Red could see Charlie's member going in and out of her, making her wild with ecstasy.

He couldn't stand the pressure of his jeans against his heavy cock anymore and he reached for the zipper. The sound of his zipper got Katherine's attention. She looked right his way. Red froze. He expected she would at least say something, if not scream. But she didn't.

She just looked at him expectantly.

Red wrapped his fingers around his erection and waited for any reaction from Katherine. She kept watching and deeply enjoying being fucked by Charlie. Red began to rub himself, responding to her gaze. He could tell it drove her crazy with excitement, being able to watch him get himself off while having another guy's hardness in her.

He was so turned on he wouldn't have been able to stop himself either. He had no idea why the whole scenario was making him so hot but it was.

"Come here," Katherine breathed and motioned him to come over.

Charlie looked surprised and confused when Red stepped to the bed but he didn't say anything. Katherine's tongue caressed her lips, signaling where he was supposed to penetrate. Her mouth was warm and she began to suck right away. Red held her head while Charlie pushed into her.

Both men moaned loudly. Red watched his friend's cock going into her body in rhythmic movements. He thrust into Katherine's mouth harder as Charlie increased the speed. Her breasts bounced in unison with Charlie's pace.

"Oh God," Charlie gasped. "I'm going to come."

Red wouldn't be able to hold it much longer either. "Oh yeah, me too," he groaned.

In a climactic frenzy, they both emptied themselves inside of their hostage.

"Don't stop!" Katherine seemed to be disappointed that it was over.

Both men grinned at each other.

"Don't worry," Red reassured her. "Charlie and I still need to swap places." He winked.

"But for now, I do need a break."

Charlie nodded in agreement. "Who wants pizza?"

5 THE SUPERGIRL

Kent was eager to arrive home. All day had been spent in anticipation of the moment when he could finally dedicate all his attention to her. He was simply crazy about her and always carried a picture of her in his wallet. He didn't find it strange, but others did. He remembered one time when his colleague Barry had snatched the billfold from him during lunch break in the cafeteria. He did things like this all the time; basically, he was just a bully. Kent always tried to ignore his cruel jokes but this day had embarrassed him. Even more so, it had hurt him. Barry found her picture and broke out in evil laughter.

"Hey guys," he yelled into the hungry crowd standing with their trays in line to get some of the horrible canteen food. "Look!" Like a glorious hero he waved the picture above his head. "Look what Kent carries around in his wallet!"

He pulled out the picture and held it still, making sure everyone could see it.

"This is his girlfriend!"

The crowd giggled, some joined in laughing at Kent, teasing him, and they wouldn't stop. For years this went on. When he ran into colleagues in the hallway they would greet him with words like, "Hey Superboy, saw your girl the other day on TV. Hot, hot, hot." And then they would burst out in laughter.

Kent was sick of it but also didn't know what to do. There was the option of forgetting about her, but he would never be able to do that. He loved her too much, even though she was just an artificial character, created after someone's imagination, drawn on paper.

"Don't worry about it," his mom would say whenever he complained about the daily harassment at work. "One day you will find the right girl and it will all be okay."

First of all, what would be okay then? Would he then forget about Tamiko? Second, how could any girl come even close to her? And third, why would any woman put up with his lifetime passion for Anime, Manga, and, ever since he was an adolescent, Hentai.

He couldn't count the number of hours he had spent in front of his computer looking at seductive pictures of girls, all designed to look innocent, young and subconsciously sexy with their naïve ignorance of their overly emphasized female attributes.

When he was younger, he couldn't wait to move out of his parents' home. He craved the video clips and movies he saw ads for on those websites he frequented. But living with his parents made it hard to watch them, much less order them. He already could picture his mom opening the package while he was at work and discovering a DVD with a front cover depicting a busty cartoon girl in teasing poses. So he had to be patient until he earned enough money to afford an apartment of his own.

The first night after moving into his own place he spent several hours at the computer trying to pick the best DVD that would offer the most pleasure. He finally found a movie starring a purple haired character with enormous breasts, a tiny waist, and seductively broad hips. The ad promised the DVD consisted of three movies presenting the girl Tamiko in different roles. What roles they didn't reveal but just the character was sufficient for Kent to click the button that read "order."

Days went by with Kent almost flying home after work to check the mail. His disappointment was crushing when it just contained some bills, if anything at all.

But then, one day he found a little brown package sitting in his mailbox. His smile went from ear to ear. That night he wouldn't let anybody interfere with his plans. He unplugged the phone, turned off his cell phone, closed the blinds, and then finally inserted the DVD into his player.

The menu came up with three movies to choose from. They didn't reveal much, only Tamiko's roles. In the first movie she was apparently a housemaid. In the second one she starred as a student, and in the third one she played a starlet. Kent examined the thumbnail of Tamiko as a maid and smiled expectantly. Yes, he would enjoy that one.

It was the story of a housemaid being used as a sex object by her employer. During the first minutes he had pulled the top of her uniform down so her voluminous breasts were exposed and had started teasing her by putting his hands between her legs. Kent was incredibly aroused. He stared at the TV while his pants were getting tighter and tighter. On the screen the employer had by now made her bend over and exposed his erected member.

"Yes," Kent mumbled, stroking the bump in his pants. "Put it in her."

The guy in the movie did, making the purple haired maid sigh.

Kent's hand slipped into his pants to reach his hardness.

The maid's employer wasn't gentle at all; he harshly pushed into her, blinded by lecherousness.

"Oh yes," Kent moaned, his hand causing his pants to stretch and relax as it moved up and down in a frenzy.

On the screen, the girl was now on top of her employer. He made her go up and down, making her full breasts bounce.

Kent's face tensed, his breathing stopped, his eyebrows contracted as his widely opened mouth released a deep and intense groan. A dark spot around the area of his hand appeared and widened while Kent's face was beginning to relax, his breath became calmer.

Recalling this first encounter with Tamiko, Kent smiled and felt his blood flowing faster through his veins. There, finally! He pulled into the driveway, parked his car and hastily scurried to his door.

Eagerly, Kent sat down in front of his

TV set, holding the remote to maneuver through the menu and pick out the best scenes of his favorite Tamiko movie. He had seen it ten times or more, he didn't really count. But he knew her every move, every sigh and every blink of her eyes. Still, every single time he saw her come up on his big flat screen he had especially bought for her, his heart started beating faster from the thrill and excitement. Or was it expectancy? Anyway, it was the same today.

Her face appeared and Kent's heart beat out of rhythm. Fascinated and with a burning desire, he stared at the girl of his dreams as she performed the same steps and actions she had done a million times before. Kent leaned back in his sofa, preparing for a hot night with Tamiko.

She reached for a toy, just like Kent had seen all those numerous times. He knew she was about to use it on herself, getting excited at this fact. But instead of grabbing the toy that lay facing the camera, she touched the screen.

Kent froze. What was that? Had he overlooked this before? He slid to the edge of the couch, both nervous and curious.

Tamiko put her head to the side as if she were examining something carefully and then her hand went through the device and became three dimensional in Kent's world, right before his eyes.

He dropped his remote in shock and kept staring at this unbelievable and unique sight. Was he dreaming? Hallucinating? Frozen with disbelief, he watched her push through the screen and stand fully formed before him. Finally he was able to move and jumped up.

"This," his finger pointed at her and the TV set alternately. "This can't be happening! This can't be real!"

But there she was, just as the artist had created her, with a ridiculously small top and an even more ridiculously short skirt.

"This is a dream, isn't it?" he asked Tamiko, hoping she would tell him what was going on. But she remained silent. She just stood there, looking at him with that innocent blush all female characters have in those drawings and animations, holding her hands folded to her side, emphasizing her shyness.

"This has got to be a dream." Cautiously, Kent reached out for her, afraid it might cause her to disappear or to go up in smoke.

His fingertips touched her arm softly but she didn't dissolve. Was it no illusion after all? He could feel her and didn't that mean that she was real? Now he let his entire hand feel her arm. It was warm beneath his fingers, her skin trembling with excitement. Yes, she was real! Kent was dizzy with excitement. He had to sit down. So he went back to his sofa and motioned Tamiko to follow him.

"Come on, I won't bite." His voice sounded weird to him, almost like the voice of a stranger.

She slowly and gracefully sat down next to him, her hair flowing smoothly, just like on the screen.

"How is this possible?" he addressed her, but she didn't say a word, she just looked at him.

Then Kent remembered. He had all of her movies and in none had she ever spoken a single word. So why would she suddenly start talking now? Suddenly, another thought crossed his mind. All she had ever done was moan, have sex, or play with toys. Did that mean that... He didn't dare follow that thought to its conclusion. But his hands started to shake in expectancy. He just had to try.

Carefully his hand approached her waist. Since she didn't react at all, neither showing agreement nor rejection, he placed his hand on it. All she did was smile shyly and blush more.

Kent couldn't believe it. He had his own playmate, right here, in his apartment. And it wasn't just any random girl. It was Tamiko. Tamiko!

"Tamiko," he whispered, his hand gliding up to her breasts.

She gave that little cute moan any

Hentai girl would give.

Kent could feel as his cock started to get stiff. Excitedly he noticed that, as he rubbed her breast passionately, her nipples got hard, too. He stopped to look at them, her top outlining the curves. Kent's fingers were eager to explore them, so he let them slide over them. Tamiko's response was a sigh.

He grew more confident and while one hand remained on her breast, his other hand slid between her legs, making her spread them a little. Kent knew from her movies what the guys had done with her, and now he wanted to take their place, acting out everything.

He began to rub her and she willingly opened her legs a little more to make it easier for him to please her. Kent could tell she was aroused as he felt her panties get wet. Encouraged by this, he rubbed harder.

As she began to knead her breasts in pleasure, he decided it was now time to do something for his own relief. Like he had done so many times before, he attempted to let his hand slide into his pants to give himself a sensual massage. But Tamiko stopped him and instead, her hand glided into his pants.

When he felt her tiny, delicate fingers fold around his rock hard erection, he let out a moan, leaning his head against the back of the couch. Her little hand gave him the most intense massage he had ever had.

With an intensity he hadn't thought possible he spilled over her hand, his member contracting many, many times between her fingers. If this was already so awesome, what would it be like to fuck her? Well, he would find out. But not tonight, he decided. He was exhausted and just wanted to fall asleep – with Tamiko in his bed.

Kent's thoughts whirled as he slowly woke up the next morning. How could he have been so stupid? How could he just go to bed? What if Tamiko wasn't there anymore?

Afraid of finding empty space next to him, he turned around slowly.

There she was, sound asleep. Kent grinned from one ear to the other. She was so hot! And she was all his!

In fascination his eyes ran over every part of her body. She was wearing panties, and only that scrap of fabric prevented him from inspecting her closely.

She was a dream, his dream, and she had been created for sex. He couldn't wait to take advantage of it. And why not now?

He was already hard again and just wanted one thing – her. So he climbed on top of her, regardless of the fact that she was sleeping. He didn't care. He had needs, incredible needs, and they had to be met in some way. That was what she was here for, wasn't it?

Having removed her panties, he grabbed his erection and, with a hard push, shoved it into her. That made Tamiko wake up but she didn't seem surprised at all.

Kent breathed heavily as he drove his hardness in and out of the girl. His old rustic bed creaked in time, Tamiko whining the same way he'd heard hundreds of times on screen.

Harder and harder he pushed into her. His hand gripped her breasts as he finally relieved himself ecstatically inside of her, yelling in a frenzy.

This was by far the best sex he had ever experienced. Hopefully she would stay with him forever. As he got out of bed to get ready for work he tried to comprehend how his life had changed during the past few hours. It was actually beyond comprehension, he concluded. How could an invented, drawn, and completely fictional character suddenly come to life? And moreover, how could she have come out of the movie, through the screen, to pop up right here in real life?

Kent fastened the belt of his pants while

he eyed his dream girl. She was still in bed, still without any clothes, and she was pleasuring herself. Her hips moved yearningly toward her hand, which slowly rubbed her cunt. Her legs were spread wide open so Kent could see everything. He cursed his work and thought for a moment to call in sick. But he couldn't do that; he needed the money. What he could do was watch for another few minutes. Turned on, his eyes followed the movements of her hand that grew faster and faster every few seconds. Tamiko moaned and Kent noticed that one of her fingers was penetrating into herself. He could only guess what it did to her, but it must have been good since her moans became louder, her hips moved in harder pushes.

Kent so much wanted to join but the clock told him to leave immediately or he would be late. With a sigh of resignation he grabbed his briefcase and headed toward the door. When he was about to lock it, he heard Tamiko scream in pleasure.

Kent smiled. When I'm back, I will be the reason for you to moan. All night. And maybe I'll bring you a toy, one of those you enjoyed so much in your movies.

With anticipation for the night to come, he got into the car and drove off.

6 I'VE GOT THE RIGHT GIRL

"Police! Open the door!" With several loud bangs Jay's fist met the white wooden door. The small golden numbers that were cheaply glued on top of the dirty white finish let visitors know that this was apartment 2001.

Since no one followed this order, it was now Craig's turn to shout. "Open the door! We know you're in there!"

And again, nothing happened. Jay and Craig exchanged a quick look before they both yelled in unison. "If you don't open the door in the next 10 seconds, we will break it down. So you'd better hurry up!"

Loud and clear they started counting down from 10, Jay looking at his watch to make sure they weren't counting too fast. "5... 4... 3... 2... 1... Go!"

The experienced officer that he was, it took Craig only a few fierce kicks with his foot and the door sprang open.

Cautiously, one after the other, with their guns at the ready, they entered the apartment.

It looked vacant. Here and there lay a few clothes scattered about, but there were no other personal items to be found. Just the empty shelves the apartment provides for their tenants.

Both officers lowered their guns.

"Are you sure this is the right apartment?" Jay asked his colleague with subtle accusation.

Craig didn't seem to notice and mumbled his response while determinedly looking for evidence. "Of course it's the right apartment! I read the warrant twice. I'm not stupid, you know?"

Jay thought it better not to say anything but his mouth revealed with a half-heartedly suppressed grin that he wasn't so sure about the latter statement.

Still grinning, he sauntered into the bathroom. Inside it was dark; there were no windows, so he had to feel for the switch.

The pale light revealed a tiny room that didn't have more than the basic equipment, namely a toilet, a sink and a bathtub with a pretty filthy shower curtain.

Jay's grin changed to disgust. "Urgh," he complained, nausea sweeping through his stomach. "No wonder no one lives here. I wouldn't even live here if I got paid for it."

Touching the curtain with only his fingertips, he pushed it back.

"What the..." He stared at his discovery in disbelief.

Crouched in the tub there was a girl, her arms wrapped around her knees. With huge, frightened eyes she stared back at Jay.

"What...," he started again, but forgot what he wanted to say while his eyes examined the girl from top to bottom. She was exactly what he wanted a woman to be like. Slim, but not too thin; long, dark hair; and a face that looked so innocent, almost childlike, with big eyes, full cheeks and a small mouth with pouted lips. 'How old is she?' he immediately wondered, since she definitely looked very young. Too young to be all alone in a shabby, run-down apartment like this.

"Hey, you found anything?" Craig yelled from another room.

That brought Jay back to reality. "Yes, indeed," he murmured.

"What's that?" Craig inquired before joining him in the bathroom. "Oh!" He seemed delighted as he saw Jay's discovery. "I guess we found our suspect."

He smiled with satisfaction as he gave the order, "Come on, Miss, get up, we don't have all day."

She obeyed and carefully got out of the bathtub, but not without defending herself. "I don't know who you are looking for, but it certainly is not me." She sounded shy and intimidated.

"Sure, sweetie." Craig grinned and signified to his partner to cuff her while he started reading her her rights.

Jay did as he was told. As he put the handcuffs around her wrists, his thoughts began to spin. He looked at her back, at her white blouse that allowed his eyes to make out her bra.

Do women wear these almost see-through blouses on purpose? Don't they know what effect it has on men? And why do they wear such short skirts?

He lowered his eyes to take a closer look at the skirt the girl in front of him was wearing. Inevitably his lips opened in slight excitement.

Skirts so short they almost reveal what's underneath.

He wished he could have made her bend over, just a little bit, to see an inch more of her beautiful legs, and maybe catch a glimpse of her hot ass, but Craig was standing right next to him. What would he think? That he was indecent, that he had lost his mind? Well, he had to admit, this girl indeed was a danger to his sanity. Her slim waist, her long hair which sweet scent he could detect, even at this distance.

"In case you wondered, my darling..." Craig's charmless laugh ended Jay's daydreams all of a sudden. "...we can't pat you down, since you are a woman. But I bet my colleague here is dying to do it anyway." His laughter echoed through the empty apartment.

"What's that supposed to mean?" Jay was angry. He always was when Craig was right about him.

"Hey man," Craig raised his hands as if to show he was unarmed. "Stay cool! It was just a joke, alright?" He shook his head in disapproval. "You don't have any sense of humor, do you know that? You are the most serious person I know."

"Listen," Jay growled. "This," he pointed at the girl. "This is not about humor. This is our job, and our job, right now, is to get this girl to the station. Do you get this or should I write it down for you?"

"What the hell is wrong with you, Jay?" Craig spat back. "Did your old lady not play with you last night?"

Alright, this was too much. Craig knew Susan and Jay broke up a few months earlier, and it wasn't pretty. She had taken almost everything – the TV, the car, even the dog. Jay was on the verge of exploding.

"You'd better get a grip, if you don't want to go home toothless!" His hand grabbed Craig's collar. "I'm not kidding," he hissed.

"Dude!" Craig freed himself from the grip. "You most certainly don't recognize a joke if it bites you in the a—"

"Get out of here!" Jay interrupted him, screaming.

Craig smiled deprecatingly. "If that's what you want, consider it done." Without another word he turned around and left.

Jay stood in silence for a moment. Did he really leave? He heard the door slam. Yes, he affirmed his question himself. And with a look to the young girl in handcuffs who was still standing quietly and without any sign of motion, it dawned on him that he not only got rid of his loathsome colleague but also was alone with this incredibly seductive girl. A shiver of happiness and excitement ran down his spine.

But what was he supposed to do – now that he was all alone with her? He would love to put his hand on her waist; he was sure he would be able to feel her soft skin through the thin fabric of her blouse. He would step closer, so his body would touch hers. And then he would let his hand slowly move to her belly, and then further up, to her breasts.

He closed his eyes and gave a sigh. Just

thinking of touching her aroused him so much he could barely stand it.

"What are you going to do with me?" He suddenly heard the girl's soft voice.

"Well," he tried desperately to calm down. "You're in handcuffs, baby, what do you think I'm going to do with you?"

Baby? Did he really say that? I will lose my job, he concluded immediately.

The girl turned her head slightly and then responded with a whisper. "I don't know, Officer." Even quieter, she added, "Will you hurt me?"

Oh dear, how was he supposed to calm down when this girl was turning him on so much? He felt his pants get tight.

"Of course not," he soothed her. But his own thoughts circled around him, unzipping his much too tight pants, lifting her skirt and...

"Oh," she said softly. "Good."

He couldn't help thinking he heard disappointment in her voice.

"I'm really not the girl you're looking for." Now she turned around to directly face him.

Her cute face stunned him, and again he wondered about her age. Was she already 18?

His eyes wandered down, to her pretty neck, to her blouse that didn't cover much of her body. If she was still underage, then she sure w very mature for her youth. He gasped while these thoughts ran through his mind.

"You certainly are the right girl," he mumbled and stepped closer to her.

For a few moments they both gazed into each other's eyes and he could have sworn the look on her face told him to just go ahead and kiss her, feel her hot breath against his skin, touch her body, her waist, her full breasts...

He was so turned on that he feared she might notice. "Alright," he said quickly and laid his hand on her back to guide her. "Let's go. The car is waiting outside."

During the entire drive Jay tried to calm himself down, to rid himself of these arousing images his mind produced. What was it about this girl that drove him so crazy? Was it her sinful mouth? Oh, it definitely was worth a sin – such full, red lips, just begging to be kissed. He pictured them touching his neck passionately, and gently moving down. Across his chest, his stomach. And they would stop right between his legs.

No! he ordered himself. This isn't professional behavior! This is wrong! Even though her lips are pretty and her breasts are... are.... And once more, his imagination went wild. He so wanted to unbutton her blouse. He would do it slowly, to maintain the tension. Then his hands would carefully touch her firm, sensual curves and start massaging them.

Will you stop it already! He got mad at himself. Why couldn't he control his thoughts anymore? He was a police officer, he belonged to the law enforcement, why was he unable to get it together?

With huge relief he noticed their arrival at the station, only to be told that he was supposed to conduct the interrogation.

"Okay, Miss..."

"Laura," she helped, shyly smiling. "Laura Morgan."

This name indeed did not match the file. It said Deborah Jenkins. But Jay didn't care much about this at the moment. He was busy trying not to picture her in his arms, sighing his name, begging him to love her.

"Age?" He couldn't even utter a complete sentence.

"23," she breathed in his direction.

"This is bound to go wrong. Very wrong," he predicted as he felt his heart race in response.

"What do you mean?" She looked at him

with confusion.

He couldn't believe it. He had said it out loud. And now? How was he to save himself now?

Patiently she waited for an answer, her eyes examining his face in detail.

"Nothing." Oh, great. Was that all he could come up with? Annoyed with himself, he shook his head.

"Why am I here?" she asked, supporting her arms on the table, slightly leaning forward.

Jay took a deep breath. The way she was sitting now allowed him a pretty deep view into her blouse. He wasn't able to take his eyes off this exciting sight.

Laura must have noticed his glance, since she bent forward even more.

Breathless, Jay mumbled, "Girl, what are you doing?"

She smiled innocently. "I really don't know what you mean."

Was she playing with him? Or did she really not know what she was doing to him?

"Don't tell me you haven't noticed," he insisted.

"Noticed what?" She crossed her leg, showing off the embroidery of her thigh-highs.

Intentional or not, this girl sure knew how to drive a man crazy, Jay noted to himself. He also leaned forward and looked her straight in the eye. With a whisper, he began his explanation.

"You've been turning me on ever since I found you in the bathtub. I'm so hot right now I can't..."

His words slowly died on him, since Laura reached for her blouse and started unfastening one button after another, watching him attentively.

"So... Do you like this?" she purred softly.

"Oh God," he sighed. "Don't... Don't do this..." His voice sounded hardly convincing, so he got up and walked over to her chair in order to emphasize he was serious. With both hands he grabbed either side of her blouse and attempted to cover her breasts she presented to him so willingly.

"If we weren't in this room here," he whispered, "I wouldn't think twice. But this could cost me my job."

She must have not listened to his words, since her hand began to caress his chest, his stomach, his thighs.

Jay had to close his eyes. He was slowly losing his mind, he feared. But it didn't matter, as long as she didn't stop.

When he felt her gentle touch between his legs, he moaned softly and opened his eyes again. "God, what are you..." His voice failed him when she slid from her chair onto her knees, unzipped his much too tight pants, and placed her lips around his extremely hard member.

"Oh God," was all he could gasp. Her mouth felt so warm and soft, her tongue teasing him playfully. He thought his knees would give out any second, so he looked for something he could hold on to. But the only thing in reach was Laura. Without further thought, he put his hand on the back of her head. She adjusted to the rhythm of his hand, and he increased the speed, forcing her head to move faster and allowing him to penetrate deeper. His breathing got harder, his moaning louder.

Laura let him go, placing her index finger on her wet lips. "Ssshh. Unless you want us to be caught." She didn't have time to point to the door, or to express another thought, before Jay pulled her up and pushed her against the wall.

"I'm gong to fuck you so hard, you won't remember your name afterwards," he promised breathlessly.

In response she pulled him closer and kissed his lips longingly.

Now he knew: she had wanted it too, the entire time! He was right when he assumed there was disappointment in her voice earlier, when he told her he wouldn't hurt her. But did that mean she was into rough sex? Well, he would soon find out, he told himself, since he was not going to be gentle. He was beyond that point now.

He already had lost control, and he needed it right now, quick, hard and dirty.

He leaned his body against hers, his left hand moving underneath her skirt to feel the firm flesh of her ass. To his pleasant surprise he couldn't feel any underwear. What he could feel, though, was her wet excitement. He was so glad she had freed his cock earlier, since by now his pants would be so tight it would probably hurt.

Slowly he began to move his hand back and forth. Laura gave a deep sigh and lifted one of her legs, her foot resting against the wall.

He increased the speed, feeling her growing lust on his hand. Her breathing was audible and she almost screamed as Jay's finger glided into her. For a few seconds, he let it stay in her, and then removed it in a torturously slow manner.

"Do you want more of this?" His voice sounded rough.

"Yes," she moaned in pleasure, moving her hips yearningly.

"You will learn not to mess with the police." Whispering these words into her ear, he thrust his hard erection into her.

This time she screamed. Jay instantly pressed his hand on her mouth.

"Shut up," he hissed, remembering what she had said earlier about being caught.

She obeyed and opened her legs as far

as it was possible for her in this position.

Jay couldn't stand it any longer. He pushed into her, faster and faster, harder and harder, staring at her breasts that bounced in his rhythm. One of his hands automatically grabbed them, massaging them violently.

"Officer," she moaned in extreme ecstasy. "I'm going to come!" Clinging to Jay's shoulders, she threw her head back and screamed again.

Jay didn't prevent her scream this time, he was busy with himself. He, too, was almost there but wanted desperately to relieve himself in her mouth.

Without saying a single word he pushed her to her knees and forced his way between her lips. Obediently, she started to suck.

"Come on, harder," he ordered. Again, she obeyed. She pressed her lips closer and used her hand for support.

That was it. He felt the explosion waving through his body, rhythmically filling her mouth with his orgasm. It was his turn to scream.

"Sssshh," Laura mumbled again. "They'll hear you."

"Doesn't matter," Jay muttered exhaustedly, trying to catch his breath. "They will see us anyway."

When Laura stared at him in confusion, he pointed at the camera that was mounted on the ceiling.

"Why didn't you say so earlier?" She obviously was upset and in a hurry to adjust her clothes.

"I just thought of it," he replied, still out of breath. "But at least this way we have a nice, vivid memory we can still watch in 30 years."

She froze and looked up to him. "You think we're still together in 30 years?"

"Who knows, anything can happen." He winked and took her hand. "Would you like some dinner, now that we have confirmed you are not our suspect?"

"But," she tried to find the right words. "I told you all along I wasn't the right girl."

"But, sweetie, you are the right girl." Softly he kissed her, before leading her out of the room.

7 ESCAPING THE FIRE

The cold was slowly creeping under her skin, into her bones. She pulled her scarf closer around her shoulders to fight the low temperatures, but it didn't provide enough warmth. The dampness of the dungeon had already soaked her linen clothes, making the cold even worse. Trembling, she crouched in a corner and rested her head against the cool stone wall.

The candle across from her was the only source of light. Father Lucius had placed it on the floor.

"This is your light," he had explained in a calm and pleased voice. "The flame of your life.

"Watch it closely. When it dies, your

time has come to climb the stake."

His piercing eyes had examined her face before he continued.

"The flames will eat you alive, Diana. First your hair."

He took a streak of her red-brown hair to emphasize his sinister explanation.

"Then it will take hold of your legs, your arms, your entire body. Nothing will be left to remember you."

He rose and looked down on her.

"No one shall remember a witch."

With these words, he left her tiny cell, making the candle flicker unsettlingly.

Why had he turned her in? She wasn't a witch; she was just an ordinary girl working as his housemaid. She had always gotten along with him, especially since she was religious. But all of a sudden, he turned against her and reported her.

She was charged with witchery, for riding a broom in the late hours around midnight, and supposedly maintaining sexual relationships with demons and the devil himself. Father Lucius had testified to seeing her engaged in making love to several creatures that had hooves instead of feet and horns on their head.

Charges like that usually meant death to the accused person, death at the stake. Diana didn't want to die. She was still so young; her entire life lay ahead of her.

With teary eyes, she looked to the candle. One third was already gone. It had been only two or three hours since Father Lucius had been in the dungeon. Four to six hours were left. That was all she had. There was no way she would be saved from the holy fires that in a few hours would be reaching for her body longingly, intended to cleanse her sinful flesh.

When she first met Father Lucius, she was 17 and homeless. Her parents had died after a long illness. She was all alone, hungry, cold, and in need of a safe place to stay. Father Lucius found her in a dirty alley and offered her a room and food, if she, in return, would keep his house clean.

He was a friendly, devout young man whose life was built around God. He taught her how to read and write, and in the evenings, after the day's work was done, they both sat in front of the fireplace, talking about the Bible.

Diana felt safe in his home, and for the first time in years, she also felt a hint of happiness. It had never occurred to her that this wouldn't last for very long. When it did end, it came so suddenly that she wasn't able to stop the events that occurred without a warning.

By the time she turned 19, Father Lucius had changed. He wasn't as friendly as he used to be. He would order her around, not leaving her a minute of rest. Diana had to work harder every week, and he was never pleased, although she gave her best. Even their Bible nights were canceled. Additionally, Father Lucius had ordered her to do strange things. Now she had to exchange her pretty dresses for what looked like rags. If she wanted to wash herself, she had to go into the barn to do so, using a wooden bowl with cold water. He wouldn't allow her to heat the water, not even in winter when the snow covered the ground inches high. And this was where she had to sleep, too, straw serving as her blanket and pillow.

"Father," she softly addressed him one morning when she fixed his breakfast.

"Yes," he mumbled gruffly. "What is it?"

"Why do I have to do those things?"

He furrowed his eyebrows.

"What things?"

"Like sleeping in the barn. Or," she grabbed the seam of the knee-length cloth she was wearing and stretched it. "Wearing this."

"Because I say so," he hissed angrily. "God disapproves of female vanity. And if a barn was good enough for Jesus, it should be good enough for you."

Diana dared raise an objection.

"But it's so cold," she explained in a quiet voice.

Father Lucius's fist violently hit the table, making the plate waiting for the breakfast to be put on it fall to the floor.

"You dare question God?"

His eyes glared with fury.

"No, I just...," she tried to defend herself, but it was too late. He grabbed her wrist and pulled her into the adjacent room, making her bend over a bench. She felt how he pulled her ragged dress up so her bare bottom would face him. He never had provided her with underwear, so she had to go without it.

"I'll teach you to obey God's word," he grumbled, right before she felt the stinging pain of something elastic hitting her behind.

Diana was too shocked to move, or even try to protect herself from the springy tree branch Father Lucius was using on her, again and again, each time with more force. She heard him groaning whenever the thin piece of wood hit her skin.

Tears welled up in her eyes. Finally, she couldn't bear the pain anymore.

"Father, please stop!" she cried with a sob.

The branch hit her one last time, causing so much pain that she released a high-pitched scream.

"This should teach you." His voice was trembling, and he was breathing heavily.

Diana didn't move. She was too scared, too afraid to look into his face, so she waited until his footsteps had faded, telling her he had left for church.

This night she wasn't able to sleep on her back, nor was it possible for her to lie on her side. Carefully, she dug her way out of the straw and went to the water bowl, where she shed her rags. Even on her hips were dark red streams. Diana didn't understand what she had done wrong, but she never wanted to experience punishment like this again.

"From now on," she whispered, raising her gaze to the ceiling. "From now on, I will be a good girl. I will prove that I'm worthy of your love."

She took a small washcloth and dipped it into the ice-cold water. This time, she was glad it wasn't hot, since the cold felt good on her wounds.

All of a sudden, Diana began to feel uncomfortable, as if there were eyes on her. As a reflex, she looked up from her maltreated body and only saw the silhouette of someone covered in a robe in the door. As soon as this shadowy creature noticed her attention, it disappeared into the night.

The next day, she told Father Lucius about this encounter. He scrutinized her intensely, and with a fierce glare he roared, "What were you doing standing naked in the barn, touching yourself, luring creatures from the underworld onto my premises!"

Diana was in disbelief over this evil allegation.

"But," she attempted to defend herself, but he wouldn't let her finish.

"Wasn't yesterday's punishment enough?" he yelled, making her shrink away. "I'll show you what we do with witches."

Twenty minutes later, she found herself kneeling in the dungeon, begging Father Lucius for forgiveness.

The flame had eaten another third of the candle's white wax. It wouldn't be long until the executioners came to pick her up. They would guide her through the town; people would stand on both sides of the street, throwing rotten fruit at her, calling her names, and demanding her slow and painful death. She had seen this happen before with other women. She had always thought they didn't look like witches or look evil at all, but Father Lucius had insisted that it was impossible to recognize a witch. He said she had to reveal herself by her actions and her talk. She hadn't questioned this—until now. Had all those women been innocent victims like her?

Her thoughts were interrupted by the creak of the door. Startled, she looked up.

Someone in a long, dark robe entered her cell. She immediately recognized it as the creature she had seen in the barn. What or who was it?

The creature walked hastily over to her.

"Who are you?" Diana asked with fear in her voice. "It isn't time yet!" She pointed to the candle.

She didn't receive an answer; the creature just took her arm and motioned her to follow him.

For several seconds Diana wasn't sure what to do. If she followed, her life might be in danger. On the other hand, it was in danger anyway—in extreme danger.

From outside, she heard the rattling of chains. The creature pulled her arm, signaling her to hurry. That was the push she needed. Without a another thought, she followed the steps of the black being.

They snuck through the narrow darkness of the sleeping town until they entered the woods and reached a lake that was securely protected from view by large rocks.

Diana sat down on the shore, exhausted. The constant fear of death she had to suffer the past hours had taken its toll. She didn't even feel the cold anymore.

"We can't make a fire here."

These were the first words the mysterious creature had spoken since they had left the dungeon, and the voice seemed just too familiar to Diana. Confused she looked up to examine the hood that draped its face in blackness.

"We would only draw attention."

"Father Lucius?" Diana gasped for breath.

A minute passed in silence, then he pulled down the hood. It was him! Diana shook her head in disbelief, staring at him with big eyes.

"Why?" she whispered, close to tears.

He didn't respond, and, avoiding her gaze, he dropped a blanket into her hands.

"So you won't be cold."

That was all he said before he climbed up a rock and made himself comfortable for the night.

Diana's head was spinning with thoughts. Why had he turned her in when, in the end, he rescued her? Was this just a game? Did he want to teach her something about God's mysterious ways? And if so, why did it have to be so brutal? Wasn't he aware that it hurt her, that she was scared to death? Wondering for hours, she finally slipped into the realms of a dreamless sleep.

When she opened her eyes, the sunlight was already warming her face. She sat up to see if Father Lucius was awake too, but he was still sleeping.

A frog croaked from somewhere close by. Diana's eyes looked for it, and when she finally spotted it, it jumped into the water. Where it dove in, the surface rippled, creating tiny circular waves.

The water looked clear and blue, just too tempting after a night of horror. Maybe Diana could sort her thoughts much better after a cool swim, washing off the dust of fear and death. She checked again to see if it was safe to undress. Yes, Father Lucius was sound asleep. Quickly and quietly, she slipped out of the ragged dress and carefully let the water touch her feet.

It was colder than she had thought, but it felt good. Carefully, she stepped into the lake, one step after another, until the water gently lapped around her waist. Diana's body stiffened as the cold sank into her skin. Slowly her hands dipped under the surface to pour some water over her arms and her upper body. With small drops, it flowed down her neck to her breasts, around her hardened nipples, to her flat belly, until it reunited with the millions and millions of drops in the lake.

She dipped her hands again to carefully run them over her breasts and her stomach, slowly adjusting to the icy temperature.

An unexpected touch made Diana flinch. There were two other hands on her waist.

"I didn't mean to scare you." Father Lucius's voice was close to her ear.

"What..." Diana stuttered. "What are you doing?"

"Taking what's mine," he breathed and softly placed a kiss on her neck.

His fingers caressed her belly and wandered up so his large hands could cover her full breasts. He moved them slightly as if to weigh them, sighing quietly into her ear.

Even though Diana was completely taken by surprise, she liked his gentle but firm touch and closed her eyes in enjoyment.

Holding her breasts with one hand, he ran his fingers down her stomach and under the surface of the lake.

Diana gave a loud moan and automatically arched her back, pressing her bottom against his loins. She sighed again as her skin touched something hard. Although she didn't have any experience, she immediately longed for it to be in her. She offered her butt even more while his hand stimulated her between her legs, softly rubbing.

Never in her life had she felt something like this. The desire was just overwhelming, her heart was racing and she wanted this feeling to be even more intense. Her hips began to move back and forth, unwittingly teasing Father Lucius.

When her hips moved back to him again, he grabbed them and, inch by inch, slid his cock into her.

She moaned in high excitement.

"Don't stop," she begged breathlessly.

"I'm not planning to," he whispered as he began to move inside of her.

All of Diana's thoughts ceased to exist. The only important thing to her at this moment was to maintain this incredible feeling. With every push, Father Lucius made it grow even stronger. As his hand massaged her breasts passionately, he sped up the rhythm of his hips, thrusting his hard erection into her.

Diana felt something building up inside of her, something she was unfamiliar with. Yet, she yearned for it. Every movement of his brought it closer to her. She had forgotten about the lake, the rocks, and the frog; she was focused only on her emotion, this feeling.

One forceful push into her, and she held her breath. Her heart was beating so fast she was afraid it might stop any moment. He pulled back and Diana reached behind her to his hips to make him push again.

Another hard push, and another. Inside of her, she felt an incredible explosion running through every part of her body in pulsing waves, making her shake and moan ecstatically. One more thrust and she felt him twitch in her, releasing hot liquid into her.

Completely exhausted, they reached the shore and laid down in the sand to let the sun dry their skin. Diana cuddled up to him and closed her eyes.

"What should we do now?" she asked, already half asleep.

"We will stay together. The rest," he put his arm around her. "We will see about that."

8 BACKSTAGE

Sandie was looking through the clothes on the rack. Nothing really seemed suitable. They were all average looking, nothing special. But it had to be special! And sexy. She wanted to be absolutely gorgeous since she only had one chance to impress him with her feminine body. Her outfit had to be an eye catcher; it had to immediately draw his attention to her. But this store obviously did not have what she was looking for. Annoyed and frustrated, she was about to leave when suddenly a light pink top caught her eye.

It looked like a corsage but it was definitely not meant to be worn as underwear. The soft pink was shimmering like silk and the edges were outlined in black color. Sandie smiled, happy to have found something for this special night when she would put all her eggs in one basket. But what should she wear at the bottom? A skirt? Pants?

The answer was found quickly. On the rack next to her top were hot pants. They were just as shiny but in a solid color – black. Sandie was delighted. The outfit problem was now solved. She would look breathtakingly sexy in these clothes, she knew it. Before heading to the checkout she paid a visit to the shoe department to choose some playful pink and black stilettos that were to be fastened around the ankles. Sandie wasn't sure if she would be able to walk in them, since they were very high, but she would risk the pain. It was worth it. For him, she would do anything.

His name was Jordan Briggs; he was Waterclay's lead singer, which made him the richest, most popular and most famous person in the music industry. He and his band had started three years ago with small gigs until a representative of a music publishing company heard them and offered them a contract. That was their breakthrough, and now, three years later, the whole world was crazy about Waterclay. Including Sandie. From the first time she had seen Jordan and heard his soft alluring voice she had wanted him. Every inch of her body longed for him, for his touch and his kisses. Late at night she would lie in bed, thinking of him, fantasizing about seducing him or being seduced by him. Often, her dreams had turned her on to this point when she couldn't help touching herself. But this had to stop, she decided. She had to get him in person. And that was what she was going to do. The concert was in one week and she would fulfill her fantasy, come what may.

At home, she tried on her new outfit in front of the big mirror in her bedroom. The corsage top had a triangular shape and reached to her slim waist, exposing the sparkling stone in her navel. Her breasts were presented in the most seductive way, only covering what was really necessary. The hot pants followed this example and left not much to the imagination. Along with her new shoes, her legs seemed even longer than they already were. Sandie examined herself from bottom to top and smiled, pleased with what she saw. He wouldn't be able to resist, she was certain. Her hands slid teasingly over her breasts, as if she was already flirting with him.

"Do you like them?" she asked her mirror image seductively, pretending it was Jordan.

"Well, why don't you touch them then?"

She increased the pressure of her

hands as they were stroking her breasts.

"That feels good," she moaned quietly, now standing with her legs apart and bending forward.

Making herself hot by pretending to turn on Jordan, her hands moved down on her body, sensually caressing her waist, her flat belly, the inside of her thighs, until one of her hands glided between her legs, applying some pressure on her sensitive area.

She gave an intense sigh, holding on to the mirror with her other hand. "Jordan." Her voice revealed high excitement, getting more and more intense as she began to move her hips like during the act of making love. Her eyes wandered to the corner of the mirror that reflected a poster of Jordan she had on her wall. Another sigh and she sank to the floor.

Kneeling and still looking at his face, her hand kept stimulating her through the fabric of her hot pants, while her hips moved back and forth, supporting the sensual feeling.

"Jordan," she whispered breathlessly. "I want you so much."

The doorbell rang. Sandie spun around, irritated and confused. Who could that be? She wasn't expecting anyone. This person better have a great excuse for jolting her out of her fantasies.

It was the mailman. But why was he

staring at her like this? Then she remembered. She was still wearing her concert outfit. How embarrassing! Especially because this guy couldn't take his eyes off her and almost began to drool. Quickly she signed the confirmation, grabbed the package and closed the door. It had finally arrived! Waterclay's last tour on DVD. The perfect thing to end an exciting day; watch the guys, and especially Jordan, perform their hits and fool around with the audience. Soon, she thought, she would be among the crowd. Just seven more days to go.

The big day was finally here. Sandie hadn't slept a wink and had left home early. No way would she let any chance of meeting Jordan pass. She had a plan, a thoroughly worked out plan. The night before she had called every hotel in this city and had pretended to be Waterclay's management. Explaining she'd made a mistake and intended to rebook, she found out that the group was staying at the Hilton. So, after the show she would definitely be there. It didn't matter that she didn't have their room numbers; she would somehow manage to find out where they were, too.

Dressed in black and pink she stood in the middle of the crowd cheering and demanding Waterclay. She had been early so she was able to get a spot right at the stage. No matter what happened next, she would not leave this spot. She needed to see Jordan from as close a distance as possible. The hall was filling up with people and the noise, the screaming and yelling became louder every minute until it was almost unbearable. Everyone in this town had been waiting for this day in anticipation. They pushed forward, but Sandie kept strong and defended her spot.

Then finally, the lights dimmed and four shadows entered the stage, all spreading out to their instruments. Music set in and the crowd went wild. The stage was lit by blue and white spotlights. All members of Waterclay were there, except for one. Jordan. The microphone had been placed in the middle of the stage, Sandie stood right in front of it. Smoke was released and covered Jordan's spot, filling the hall with a sweet smell. As it dissolved Sandie's heart stopped for a minute and she thought she was going to faint. There he was! Jordan! Her Jordan! Right in front of her, singing the first line of "Whatever You Do," their first hit single.

Come on, she told herself, pinching her arm. Sandie, you won't pass out! You aren't here to faint, but to see him.

Longingly, she looked up to Jordan's face. He looked even better than on TV or on the posters on her wall. His hair was as black as hers; his blue eyes could pierce steel and melt every woman's heart. Sandie lost herself in that amazing blue, so that several songs went by without her noticing. When he started his usual fooling around with the band and the audience, his eyes met her gaze.

Sandie froze. He was looking at her! He was staring right into her eyes! Was this happening? Could he see her?

She felt disappointment rush through her body. Probably not. It was much too dark and the stage lights were much too bright. He probably wasn't even aware that he was looking at her.

Jordan seemed to support her assumption by turning around and talking to some security guy before stepping up to his microphone again to start a new song. It was "Love Me Always," a wonderfully kitschy ballad. Sandie lost herself again in his velvet-like voice and his hypnotic eyes.

The songs flew by and all of a sudden it was time to go. Sandie couldn't believe it was already over. It hadn't even begun! They had just played a few songs! But when she took a look at her cell phone she realized it had been three hours.

Wow, she thought in amazement. It's weird that I didn't even notice the pain in my feet.

She looked down to her stilettos and smiled a bittersweet smile. Even though she planned on going to the hotel to try to get close to Jordan, she also knew her chances were pretty slim. But she would try. After all, she hadn't bought her outfit for nothing.

As she slowly walked toward the exit, someone from the security team stepped in her way.

"Wait a second, Miss," he grunted and eyed her carefully.

"What's wrong?" Sandie couldn't understand why he would stop her. She hadn't done anything wrong. Or, had she?

He didn't answer. "Follow me, please."

Sandie felt fear creeping up to her throat, making it hard for her to talk without trembling.

"But, why? What's wrong?"

"Nothing is wrong," he tried to reassure her but his deep voice sounded too aggressive as that Sandie would have believed him. "Will you please follow me?"

He didn't wait for a response but grabbed her arm and pushed her gently forwards.

"Where are we going?" Sandie kept inquiring, being on the verge of panicking, as he led her through a narrow hallway.

He remained silent the next few seconds, and then he stopped in front of a door.

"Here we are," he announced.

Sandie read the sign on the door. "Dressing Room Waterclay – Jordan Briggs".

Helpless and in absolute disbelief, she turned to the security guy, opening her mouth to say something, but words failed her.

The guy just smiled and opened the door to let her in.

"Have fun," he winked before he left her standing there alone.

Her heart was close to a cardiac arrest. Sandie could feel it. It was racing, pumping blood unusually fast through her system.

What was she supposed to do? Should she just enter? Or she could still run away, it wasn't too late yet.

"Hey," she heard an eerily familiar voice addressing her.

Slowly she raised her head to see Jordan in the room, standing just opposite from her, smiling.

"Why don't you come in?"

Yes, why didn't she? Taking a deep breath, she took a step forward.

Jordan laughed, his voice friendly.

"You're still not in my room."

He walked over to her and took her hand, his fingers folding around hers. Sandie prayed he wouldn't notice how much she was shaking. But he did. Surprised, he looked into her eyes.

"Are you afraid of me?"

Quickly she shook her head.

"I'm just nervous," she stuttered, smiling with a blush.

He returned her smile and softly pulled her in his dressing room.

"Sandie." He spoke her name as if he wanted to try its taste on his tongue. "That's a beautiful name." He smiled warmly. "For a beautiful girl."

The butterflies in Sandie's stomach were tumbling around heavily. Here she was, in Jordan's dressing room, sitting right next to him on his couch.

"You know what?" he asked quietly.

Sandie shook her head, hanging on his every word.

"I saw you standing at the stage when I was singing."

She blushed deeply and lowered her head. So he had seen her.

His index finger lifted her chin to make her look at him again.

"I just had to meet you. You are so..." His voice got quiet and he slowly leaned closer to her.

"You are so... so...," he tried again in a

whisper, his mouth just an inch from her lips.

Sandie was dizzy with excitement.

"So... what?" she whispered back with a look on her face that told him she was his already.

His lips touched hers and he closed his arms around her body, pressing her against him, kissing her more forcefully and making her get on his lap.

Sandie's mind stopped working. All she could focus on now was Jordan. She wanted him so badly.

He apparently felt the same way, since his hands were stroking her back, her butt that was only half covered by her pants, while his kisses became more demanding. Sadie's hips automatically started to move teasingly on his lap.

"Oh baby, you're driving me crazy," he breathed heavily into her ear, grabbing her butt to make her move harder.

Sandie sighed in response. She could feel that he was aroused and she yearned for him to be in her. "Jordan, I want it so much."

She didn't need to tell him twice. With his entire body weight he forced her down on the sofa, with him on top. Hastily he pulled down her pants and unzipped his. His erection was immense and Sandie just had to touch it.

Jordan gasped. "You want to put it in

you?"

The thought of having control over his penetration made her even hotter and carefully she led him to herself. Inch by inch he went into her, filling her completely.

"This feels so good, baby," he moaned deeply as he began to move his hips, pushing his hardness deep into Sandie.

She bent her knees a little more, lifting them up to her head and spreading her legs wide so he could glide even deeper into her. They both gave a groan.

But it wasn't intense enough for Sandie. She lusted for more.

"Jordan, please, I need it harder."

His hips adopted a faster, fiercer rhythm, thrusting his erection forcefully into her. Her sighs became louder and with every hard push their volume increased until she nearly screamed.

"Are you coming?" he asked, blind with lust.

His moving in and out of her, his constant stimulation of her sensitive spot was impossible to withstand any longer.

"Yes," she yelled ecstatically. "Oh yes, Jordan."

Waves of the highest excitement ran through her body, making her shake and scream his name. Her climactic contractions massaged Jordan's member and made him come too. He threw his head back, moaning and pouring heavily into her.

Exhausted, he lowered his head again and let his mouth look for her ear. "Just to let you know. I'm not finished with you yet. We don't have another gig tomorrow, so I'm planning to spend that time in my hotel room, doing you until we both don't remember where or who we are."

Sandie smiled in anticipation and happiness. She couldn't wait to explore and reach every possible sexual gratification. And moreover, it would be with the man of her dreams. Jordan.

9 CONSOLATION PRIZE

Richard took another sip of his whiskey. This whiskey was elected to be his lifesaver tonight. Grimly, he held the bottle in his hand and read the label as if he had never seen it before. Habit, probably. He weighed the bottle with this invaluable liquid manually and decided it was time for another one. He shuffled across the small hotel room to the cupboard that displayed his shopping from earlier today, right after he came out of court. Another four bottles of Johnnie Walker and one bottle of some swill he had spotted at the store.

Why not, he had thought. As long as it keeps me from reality, anything goes.

Richard had lost today. Even though he was so well prepared, he had lost.

His hands twisted the cap off his drink and he eagerly poured it down his throat.

He was a good lawyer. Actually, he was a great lawyer. The wealthiest clients would carry their cases to his office. Not to anyone else's, no, to his! But that was over now. He was sure of it. With a dirty spot on his reputation like the one he received today, no one would even bother to dial his number. He could already hear people gossiping.

Richard Brooks? No way am I going to call him! Haven't you heard about the Wilson case?

The Wilson case. He wouldn't have guessed in years that this would break his neck. Well, it did. What an embarrassing, pathetic end to his career. Even the district attorney smiled dismissively.

He took a big swig of his beloved whiskey. The world around him began to spin. This was the moment he had been waiting for. Now he was starting to relax. But he couldn't forget. His mind kept taking him back to the courthouse, to the audience staring at him pitifully, to his client who not only lost thousands of dollars today because of him but also his freedom. For five years. Before, people referred to him as the miracle lawyer who could bail out anyone. Not today. He couldn't bail out Wilson.

"Stop it," he hissed, shaking his head

fiercely as though he could shake out the day and its memories. He drank some more and walked over to the telephone on the nightstand. He didn't want to be alone now. Usually his wife would try to cheer him up but she wasn't here. She was at home watching the kids.

His fingers dialed his best friend's number. The signal rang in his ear.

"Yep?"

Richard had to grin. His friend always answered the phone like this, even at work.

"Didn't go so well," he slurred into the phone.

"Aw no, what happened?"

"Lost. It's all over now." Richard's words were almost unintelligible.

"Come on, don't say that. You're a hell of a lawyer and you know it."

"Nah, it's over," he repeated and put the bottle to his mouth.

"You need something to cheer you up, Rick. How about a girl?"

"I'm married," he responded after taking another drink.

There was a sigh at the other end of the line.

"What?" Richard inquired.

"Believe me, a girl will make you forget about this. You'll feel better in no time. Let me find the number for you."

A few moments of silence followed until

Rick's friend happily announced that he had found it.

"Get a pen and write it down," he ordered.

"Alright," Richard murmured and scribbled the number on one of the papers he had used in court today.

"Call, okay? You won't regret it."

"Uh-hm," he nodded before he hung up, not thinking about the fact that his friend had been unable to see his nodding.

He took one more sip and studied the part of the paper that provided the promising number. Should he call?

What the hell, he shrugged and picked up the phone again. Why not.

"Hello, this is Candy. How may I help you?" He was immediately greeted with a syltry voice.

"Um..." Rick wasn't sure. "A friend gave me this number and..."

"Oh, I see," the almost exaggeratedly sexy voice purred through the receiver. Richard heard her smiling. "Well, tell me about the type of girl you prefer and I will do my best to help you."

He told her he liked girls that were slim but well endowed, that had long hair and even longer legs. And if possible, with not much on. He had to laugh at his latter remark. Obviously, no man really did like clothes on women, right?

Unimpressed, Candy explained that she

would send a girl to his hotel room, thanked him for calling and hung up.

"Send me a girl," he repeated mockingly. "I bet she's a dog. And what am I supposed to do with her anyway?"

Richard poured some more whiskey down his throat and made himself comfortable on the bed, surrounded by a supply of liquor bottles.

He didn't have to wait long until he heard a knock on the door.

"Come in," his deep voice slurred uncontrollably.

The girl sent by Candy entered his room, closed the door behind herself, and kept standing there.

Richard's jaw dropped. She wasn't a dog at all. Her face was almost doll-like, framed by cute brown curls. But what was wrong with her outfit? It was more like a business suit than anything else.

"Are you okay with me?" the young girl asked shyly.

"Sure," he mumbled, still stunned. "But what is this?" His index finger pointed at her clothes.

"Oh," she smiled, blushing. "Well, did you want everyone to know why I'm visiting you?"

Richard nodded. Yes, that made sense.

"But now you're here, so..."

He waited for her to complete the sentence herself. Let's see how far I can go with her, he thought, still not thinking about cheating on his wife.

She understood and one by one, she unfastened the buttons of her blue blazer, revealing a red bra that was extremely well-filled.

For the first time Richard contemplated sex with her. She definitely turned him on, even though he was as drunk as he could be. Surprisingly, his best part did still react to this gorgeous female.

She dropped the blazer and started unbuttoning her pants.

Hell, Richard exclaimed in his head. Is she wearing a garter belt?

Her pants fell on top of the blazer. Yes, she was wearing a garter belt; a red one to match her bra. With red stockings and a red G-string.

"You like it?" she asked professionally.

Richard swallowed hard. "Yeah," he whispered, staring at this hot sight in front of his bed with hungry eyes. Desire began to well up inside him; the desire to have her, to possess her, to dominate her all night.

His wife didn't like his fantasies. He had once asked her to play along but she firmly refused, expressing her disgust with his wishes. She wouldn't even wear a garter belt. He loved her but he also was a victim of his desires. So maybe tonight he had his lifetime chance to fulfill his dreams.

With his index finger he motioned the girl to come over to him. Right next to the bed he signaled her to stop.

"I figured I should tell you in advance." He carefully examined her face for any sign of disgust or rejection. "I like it rough. I don't want to ask your permission to do things, I just want to do them. Whatever it is. I want you to be submissive to me tonight. I want you to do as you're told. If you have a problem with this, you'd better go now."

He waited for a minute and watched her reaction. She stood still and nodded, agreeing to what he had proposed.

"Tonight, I'm yours, willing to do whatever you want." She looked at him seductively.

Richard was on cloud nine. Was this really happening? He needed to test it.

"Get on this bed and kneel in front of me," he ordered excitedly.

Would she do it? His head spun as he realized she was doing as she was told.

Kneeling at his feet, she eyed him expectantly.

With a thrill of anticipation that ran through his body, he sat up so his back could lean against the wall. This way he could watch her better.

"Touch yourself... and get rid of this annoying bra!" He almost shouted his order in excitement.

Withstanding his lustrous gaze, the girl began to knead her voluminous breasts.

Richard's mouth dropped open, aroused by her play.

Her hands glided along the sides of her breasts, pushing them together so they bulged out of the bra. She leaned a little bit forward to make it easier for Richard to see.

He was pretty sure his pants had never felt so tight. Inevitably he ran his hand over the clearly visible bump in his pants, applying some pressure.

"Mmh," he groaned quietly. That felt good.

The girl's hands slid further, between her breasts, to unfasten her bra. As soon as it was loose her big breasts popped out and she threw it behind her.

He had never seen such voluptuous curves, he noted to himself, almost drooling.

"Come on, what are you waiting for? Play with yourself," he instructed, his voice trembling with lecherousness.

She obeyed and let her hands move over her breasts, down her flat belly, into her G-string. Richard received a mischievous smile before one of her hands returned to her breasts while the other one remained in her panties and began to caress herself. Her eyes shut, she put her head back, softly sighing. She obviously enjoyed this game. Her hips started to move back and forth, increasing the volume of her breath.

"Yes," Rick encouraged her, slowly continuing to massage the bump between his legs. "Show me what you do when you're home alone."

She began to rub herself harder, her hips adjusting to the faster rhythm. Her lips released moans of pleasure.

Blind with yearning, he unzipped his pants and got up. He just had to do something about his erection which was by now so hard it almost hurt.

He stood on the bed, right in front of the girl.

"Open your mouth," he demanded.

Richard placed a hand behind her head and pulled it toward him, forcing her to embrace his hardness with her lips.

He groaned ecstatically and remained still, enjoying the feeling of being in her mouth. The girl's tongue started to tease him gently, while her hand was still in her G-string, moving fiercely. All of a sudden she froze, even her breath stopped. She made a sound that came close to whining, her body shaking all over.

"You just came, didn't you?" he gasped

breathlessly.

Richard pulled halfway out of her mouth, before he eagerly pushed in it again. She pressed her lips tighter around him as Rick pushed her head back and forth.

With a long, deep moan he came hard in her mouth, holding her head close so she was forced to swallow.

When she attempted to withdraw he pulled her back.

"Not so fast, baby. I'm not finished with you yet."

With a strong pull, he tore off her G-string.

"Do me," he ordered harshly after he had sat down again and leaned back against the wall.

She hesitated and looked at him helplessly.

"Do me," he repeated impatiently and grabbed her wrist to pull her on his lap.

He felt his erection slowly going in her; she tightly embraced his hardness.

"That's good," he whispered. "Now move. Do me real good, baby."

Her pelvis started to move in slow circular motions, rubbing herself against him.

"Come on, you can do better." His hands grabbed her butt and guided her movements, making them faster and harsher. Fascinated, he noticed that her breasts adopted this rhythm, too. He couldn't take his eyes off them while his member received a massage due to her muscles and her riding him.

Her nails suddenly scratched his shoulders, her body getting stiff.

"Oh God," she uttered, shaken by another climax.

"Don't you think about it," Richard hissed. "Don't stop."

His hands forced her to continue the rhythm, supported by his hips pushing toward her.

"Faster," he ordered, spanking her harshly.

The girl gave a sigh of surprise and did as he wished.

Rick could tell it turned her on, he could feel it inside her. He spanked her again. She rubbed against him with quicker motions. Again, his hand landed on her bottom, making her moan.

"You like that, don't you?"

She nodded and did him harder every time he hit her.

One more spank and she let out a scream, holding on to her breasts, shivering and shaking.

"Don't tell me you came again," Richard warned amusedly.

She had. Completely exhausted, she sank into the sheets, breathing hard.

"Not yet." He robbed her of the hope of

some rest.

Richard turned her on her stomach and with one hard push he thrust into her, causing her to moan.

"Sorry," he mumbled. "I will make it quick."

Having said that, he went in and out of her almost violently, spanking her and the closer he came to his orgasm, the more names he called her.

"You dirty whore, I'm going to squirt inside you," he yelled, just before he exploded in her.

Tired but satisfied, he got off her and reached for his wallet. He picked out a bundle of bills and threw it onto the bed, next to her, before he slipped into a dreamless sleep.

Richard woke up with a pounding headache.

"Oh God, no more alcohol. Ever."

He blinked into the sunlight coming in through the blinds. He would definitely need an aspirin if he wanted to drive home today to his family. The thought of his wife caused his conscience to well up. And then, slowly but surely, last night's memory returned.

He had enjoyed it but how could he ever

look into Sarah's eyes again? Not to mention his kids.

He checked his cash. 600 dollars? Was he out of his mind? He had paid her 600 dollars? Angry with himself, he got up to take a hot shower. Maybe that would chase the clouds in his head away.

Unfortunately, it didn't. He ended up having to take two aspirins before he got into his car. At home, Sarah was already awaiting him with questions.

He didn't want to tell her how it went. He didn't want to tell her that his career was now over. And by no means did he want to tell her how he completely let himself go and screwed a prostitute several times. But she had been awesome. Her body was every man's dream.

He looked at his wife and suddenly was hit with the image of her cheating on him. Was it possible? He did something he hadn't done in a long time – he examined her body closely.

Sarah had hair the color of hay that fell to her waist and framed her face beautifully. She was conservatively dressed with a pastel pink sweater and jeans, but it didn't stop Richard from making out her curves. Like the prostitute from last night, she, too, was slim and well-endowed. How could he have forgotten how beautiful his wife was? How could he have forgotten just how desirable she actually is?

Richard reached out to cup her cheek and kissed her softly on the lips. Her scent hit him fully and he felt desire course through his body. He put his arms around her and held her close, letting her feel his hardness.

Surprised, but willing, Sarah let him guide her to the kitchen counter where he lifted her up and sat her down without breaking from the kiss. She could feel the sadness and a hint of desperation behind the kiss and wondered what could've happened.

"What's gotten into you?" she asked as she started unbuttoning his shirt. She may not be the most sexual of women, but she wasn't unfeeling. And she felt desire for her husband as he kneaded her breasts and thumbed her nipples. She felt herself getting wetter and wetter.

Richard's hands travelled lower to unbutton her jeans. He removed them along with her white lace panties, exposing her long, milky legs. He clenched his jaw as he tried to regain some control over his primal urges. Richard reached out to his wife and tilted her head so that he could kiss her neck, fighting the urge to bite the flesh.

"Richard..." Sarah moaned, gripping his bare shoulders and encircling her legs around his waist. She couldn't take it anymore and whispered in his ear. "Hurry."

He lacked the patience needed to remove his pants completely, so he unzipped them instead and pulled his underwear down enough to take out his cock, already glistening with pre-cum at the tip.

Sarah bit her lower lip as she felt her husband's cock being positioned at her entrance. They moaned loudly as Richard gave one hard thrust that sent Sarah reeling with pleasure. The fact that they were making love in the kitchen and that she was fully exposed while Richard was only half-naked only added to the thrill. She gave a small thrust upward, goading Richard into moving. He made short, quick thrusts as he was in no mood to prolong the pressure that was building and building in his cock. Sarah didn't seem to mind; in fact, she seemed to welcome his hurry as she gripped his shoulders tighter, moaning louder and louder each time their hips met.

Sarah came first, arching her back and scraping her nails almost painfully on Richard's skin. Her insides convulsing around his cock was what made Richard cum, and cum inside her he did. He held her close to him as they both trembled from the aftershocks of orgasm.

"Did something happen while you were

away?" Sarah asked, wiping the sweat from Richard's brow.

"Not really," he replied. "It's just so good to be home."

10 IN DARKNESS HE WALKS

Alice slowly turned around, intimidated. She could swear someone was looking at her. Someone close by... but there was nobody, not a soul. She was alone, all by herself in the castle. Somehow, she wished she hadn't been this confident in herself and chosen to come here after dark. She'd believed the atmosphere would be breathtaking and would sharpen her senses for anything inexplicable—anything paranormal. The atmosphere was definitely breathtaking, but not like what she had expected—or what she had hoped for it to be. Instead, she was incredibly terrified and her senses were obviously playing tricks on her.

She couldn't tell how many minutes or even hours she had spent on the upper floor. But she knew she was getting paranoid. There! Were those footsteps? She cringed. Oh, it was the sound of her own footsteps. She had taken a step back, unconsciously, causing the sound of her heels to echo through the huge, empty hall.

The room she was standing in offered nothing: nowhere to seek shelter, nothing that would help calm down an upset spirit. Except for some large oil paintings on the wall and two cushioned chairs, there was no place for reassurance, not even some candles waiting to be lit. Darkness made it impossible for Alice to make out the color of the images, but she could just make out the subject of the pictures. Not in detail anyway but she could see that they were portraits. Portraits like those one can find in any royal home. They probably depicted the family that lived here a long time ago.

Alice tried to remember the family's name. Before she came here, she had read about them comprehensively. Wasn't it Rogues? And weren't all the family members killed by a mysterious disease that had led to a lot of blood loss? Therefore, the myth that they were turned into vampires and now still inhabited this castle was formed. It was also said that only fools would set foot into these walls. Maybe she was one of those fools. Right now she definitely felt like one.

Alice took a deep breath to calm down and stepped closer to the wall. The image she was standing in front of showed a rather handsome man in a suit and bow tie. His face must have been painted in a very light color since it stood out against the blackness of the night.

What was that? Alice jumped back in horror, releasing a high-pitched scream. The eyes had moved! She had clearly seen it. The eyes of the man in this painting had moved! Alice was trembling in fear, unable to move. She stared at the gold-framed picture, hoping it was just an illusion.

But no! There it was again! The eyes moved to the right!

Alice panicked and ran towards the stairs. She almost fell down the steps but got a hold of the railing. She took several steps at once until she was in the entrance hall and headed toward the door.

It was locked! Alice pushed it violently and tried to pull it, shake it, and even kick it. The heavy wooden door remained locked.

A cool breeze blew through the hall and made her shiver. She only wore a light summer dress and wasn't prepared for a cold night in an English medieval castle, right in the middle of nowhere. There weren't any buildings close by, so if she screamed for help, no one would hear her. Alice began to rue the day she decided to fly to the United Kingdom. She did it just out of curiosity and fascination for the dark. She loved the legends about hauntings and vampires. But now she could very well do without them, and she had more darkness than she wanted. One last time she tried to push open the door. The wood just creaked; that was all that happened. She was trapped.

The windows were protected by black metal bars, which prevented robbers from climbing into them and plundering the riches of the royal family that once had inhabited the castle, but right now they also prevented Alice's escape.

She sank to the cold stone floor and began to weep. She wanted to get out of this place; it was cold, dark, and scary, and she felt she wasn't alone, even if she didn't see anyone. But the eyes of the painting haunted her and she still felt them on her.

Was she starting to lose her mind? What was wrong with her? After all, it was just an abandoned castle. She had never been afraid of the dark and never believed those ghost stories. So, why in the world did it terrify her so much now?

She winced. Was there a shadow moving past her? She saw it clearly, but she quickly dismissed it again as being a trick of her mind.

There! There it was again, flying right toward her!

Alice screamed in terror as she crawled backwards into a corner and huddled up to the stone walls as if they could offer protection.

She froze as the shadow echoed her scream, but it didn't sound human. It sounded more like an animal, like a rat or... or....

Alice forgot how to breathe. Was it really possible? All the legends she had read had talked about bats—bats that turned into humans, or actually vampires.

The shriek faded, as did the shadow. It just dissolved. Alice looked around but no shadow was to be seen, other than hers, which was created by the dim light of the full moon.

Full moon! Alice jumped to her feet at once, recalling all the myths and horror stories she had ever heard, comparing it to what she was experiencing tonight. The moving eyes in the picture, the locked doors, the feeling of being watched, the shadow, the animal sound, a full moon!

Panic flowed through her system. Out! her inner voice yelled at her. Out! Get out of here! She ran toward the stairs again. Maybe there was a balcony on the first floor. If it wasn't too high, she could climb down and flee. Her heart raced in excitement of the new hope. It wasn't much but enough to encourage her to try.

Another scream tore the air. It was suffused with tears, hopelessness, and deadly terror. Only as it stopped did Alice realize it was herself. A tall black figure had suddenly appeared on the bottom of the steps and held his arms wide open, as if to hinder her from going upstairs.

Alice's eyes flooded with tears, which ran down her cheeks.

"Please," she cried in despair, dropping to the hard floor. "Please."

She didn't know what she was pleading for.... Her life? Her freedom? Her sanity? She just knew she wanted this to end. She couldn't take this enormous fear much longer; it would drive her crazy.

Alice was met with silence. As she looked up, still shaken with tears, she found the stairway empty. What was going on? Was this all in her mind? She decided to retreat to her corner and wait for sunrise. Daylight made everything look different.

She wasn't sure how long she had slept but she recalled having nightmares. A creature with huge fangs had held her in its arms, mumbling words she didn't understand. It had finally placed her on a bed, and before it left, it had touched her neck. "Soon" was a word she did understand. Surprisingly, it hadn't scared her. In her dream she was indifferent to the things that happened to her... but now that the memory came back, she shivered. Was it already daylight?

Alice sat up to look out of the window—and froze. This wasn't the entrance hall! This room didn't have any windows and it was much smaller. And she was sitting on a bed! Alice tried to make out the door in the darkness without success.

There must be a door! So where was it?

Anxiously she got up and felt for any sign of the door in the wall that would lead outside. But there were none!

"This is a dream," she mumbled to herself, almost panicking. "This is just a dream. A bad one but I'm going to wake up. Nothing but a dream."

The cool breeze she had felt before blew through this room. Alice hugged herself in an effort to keep herself warm, and then, out of thin air, a black figure materialized.

Shocked, Alice backed up against the wall, seeking shelter that was nowhere to be found in this damned castle.

As before, the creature spread its arms, revealing what seemed to be either wings or a wide coat.

"Don't," the figure said. Even though it was a whisper, Alice felt intimidated by its authority and the fact that its voice seemed to consist of echoes. She couldn't tell if the voice was high or if it was deep. It harbored all tones in itself, sounding like from another world.

"Don't," the voice repeated as its wings closed in on her.

Strangely, Alice didn't question the command, since she suddenly knew what it meant. This creature wanted her to be calm, without fear, and she knew it wouldn't hurt her.

As these thoughts ran through Alice's head, she could feel the figure smile. She didn't see its face nor did she hear anything, but something within her told her it smiled.

The room was beginning to turn brighter. Alice automatically raised her head to inspect the ceiling but there wasn't any source of light, there or on the walls.

The brighter it became, the more she could see the creature. The last shadow vanished and gave way to a smooth, handsome male face. Immediately, Alice was captivated. Why had she been so afraid all the time? Her heart was racing but this time it wasn't terror that made it beat so fast. Alice lost herself in these twinkling, fiery red eyes. She didn't even stop to wonder about the color. To her it was as normal as anything.

"I've been watching you." His voice was hypnotizing. "You caught my attention when you entered my castle. A lot of people have been here, but no one like you."

He stepped closer before he continued. Alice could just stand there and listen with fascination to his alluring voice.

"You are beautiful." His cold hand on her cheek made her shiver, but not because of the cold. What was it about him that made her so weak? His words didn't even reach her. Was it his perfect face? His tall stature? Or was it his hypnotic voice?

With a movement so fast she wasn't able to see it, he had grabbed her and was now pushing her against the wall.

"You have sparked the flame of desire in me," he whispered, explaining his actions. "And now I'm making you mine."

Alice could just think of one thing: "Yes, please, I want to be yours." Willingly, she sank into his arms and let him kiss her lips with a fierce passion.

His kiss felt warm, not as cold as his touch. Alice felt it run through her entire body, charging it with electricity. Never before had she experienced something that even came close to this. This feeling was just overwhelming; she didn't want it to stop. She wanted more of it. Eagerly she received his kisses that seemed to completely burn her.

"No," she sighed desperately, reaching for him as he distanced himself.

A mischievous smile spread across his face that bared his long, pointed fangs.

Instead of shrinking away, Alice felt the deep need to be close to him. Otherwise, she would perish. "Soon," he promised, right before he disappeared.

Alice lay on the bed. She had spent hours trying to figure out what had just happened. She almost gave herself to... to.... What was he? Could it be possible that he was a... vampire? It was ridiculous! But his eyes, his teeth, his voice: all these pointed to the fact that he indeed was a creature of the night. Or maybe it was just her imagination, but then again, for an imagination, he had felt extremely real. Just the thought of his kisses made her close her eyes yearningly.

She pictured him touching her, kissing her deeply, and holding her tight. Slowly and smilingly, she drifted into the sweet land of sleep.

In her dreams, he came back and lay down next to her. He kissed her with as much desire as she felt for him. His kisses, she thought in her dream, could burn up her soul. It definitely was on fire and he was the only one to douse it. Stronger and stronger grew her will to be his completely. What was it he did to her? Had he bewitched her or put her under some love spell?

She gave an ecstatic moan as his icy fingers embraced her breast and gently started playing with it. Under his touch she squirmed and writhed, begging him for more.

Softly he covered her body with his, embracing her with his wings.

Her desire got too much for her to handle in this dream and she opened her eyes, only to stare right into the glowing red eyes that belonged to the body she so much yearned for. Had it not been a dream?

He kissed her and all her thoughts ceased to exist. Her brain stopped working entirely; she could only focus on him.

How it happened, she couldn't tell, but she felt that the fabric between her legs was missing. Until now, she had worn a thong under her white summer dress, but all of a sudden, she didn't feel it anymore. It was gone. Instead, she felt that he was aroused, at least as much as she was.

"You will be mine," he purred with his irresistible voice.

Alice felt him penetrating her, hard and stiff. The intensity of him entering her was so overwhelming that she thought she was going to die any second. To her actual surprise, it didn't happen, but she learned that it was indeed possible to heighten this almost unbearably intense feeling. With a few deep pushes inside of her, he made her climax so hard that she scratched his entire back with her fingernails. He didn't seem to mind and kept moving in and out of her, faster and faster, until he exploded inside her, burying his fangs in her neck.

Alice came for the second time. This time the intensity of her orgasm was so strong her heart stopped.

"You will be mine forever," were the last words she heard alive. Her heart failed to beat again, and her skin turned pale as he voraciously drained her of her sweet red juice of life.

It must have been several hours since

she had died when she suddenly could perceive the hoot of an owl outside. Cautious and dizzy, she opened her eyes.

He was right beside her, admiring her beauty.

"Now you are mine." He smiled innocently.

Strange, Alice thought. His voice is so different. So normal....

"It's not," he replied, amused. "It's you who are different. You have just entered the gates of eternity."

"You can read my mind?" Alice was startled. "And what do you mean by eternity?"

Softly he caressed her neck. "Of course I can. You can read mine too, if you try. You are now like me." He bent over her to kiss her lovingly. "You are now my bride for all the time there is to be."

AUTHOR'S NOTE

Readers: I want to expand a few of the stories to see where the characters can be explored further. If there are any of the stories that you would like to read more about again, I'd love to hear from you!

Visit my blog at www.helanaparkins.com

Join my newsletter for free exclusive previews
www.helanaparkins.com/in

Follow me on Twitter at
www.twitter.com/helanaparkins

Like my page on Facebook at
www.facebook.com/helanaparkins

Discover my books at major ebook retailers everywhere.